W9-BJC-575

Hot Hand

Hot Hand

a Comeback Kids novel

MIKE LUPICA

SCHOLASTIC INC.
New York Toronto London Auckland Sydney
Mexico City New Delhi Hong Kong Buenos Aires

No part of this publication may be reproduced, stored in a
retrieval system, or transmitted in any form or by any means,
electronic, mechanical, photocopying, recording, or otherwise,
without written permission of the publisher. For information
regarding permission, write to Philomel Books, a division of
Penguin Young Readers Group, a member of Penguin Group
(USA) Inc., 345 Hudson Street, New York, NY 10014.

ISBN-13: 978-0-545-09464-1
ISBN-10: 0-545-09464-X

Copyright © 2007 by Mike Lupica. All rights reserved.
Published by Scholastic Inc., 557 Broadway, New York,
NY 10012, by arrangement with Philomel Books, a division of
Penguin Young Readers Group, a member of Penguin Group
(USA) Inc. SCHOLASTIC and associated logos are trademarks
and/or registered trademarks of Scholastic Inc.

12 11 10 9 8 7 6 5 4 3 2 1   8 9 10 11 12 13/0

Printed in the U.S.A.   40

First Scholastic printing, November 2008

Design by Gina DiMassi
Text set in Bookman

This book is for my sister, Susan.

ACKNOWLEDGMENTS

My thanks, as always, to those who so generously read my books as they are being written: my wife, Taylor; Esther Newberg; William Goldman; Susan Burden; and, of course, Michael Green.

And, as always, I thank the children whose spirit runs through all these books: Chrisopher, Alex, Zach and Hannah.

ONE

It had been three days since Billy Raynor's dad told them that he was going to live in a different house.

His mom explained that it was something known as a "trial separation."

Yeah, Billy thought, a separation of thirteen blocks—he'd counted them up after looking at the map in the phone book—plus the train station, plus the biggest park in town, Waverly Park, where all the ballfields were.

His parents could call it a "trial separation" all they wanted, try to wrap the whole thing up in grown-up language, the way grown-ups did when they had something bad to tell you. But they weren't fooling Billy.

His dad had left them.

Now his mom was leaving, too.

She wasn't leaving for good. It was just another one of her business trips, one Billy had known was coming. She'd told him and his sister and his little brother that she had to go back up to Boston for a few days because of this big case she was working on. A *real* trial, instead of a dumb trial separation. That was why it was no big surprise to him that her suitcases were in the front hall again, lined up like fat toy soldiers. And why it was no surprise that the car taking her to the airport, one that looked exactly like the other long, black, take-her-to-the-airport cars, was parked in the driveway with the motor running.

Another getaway car, Billy thought to himself, like in a movie.

From the time his mom had started to get famous as a lawyer, even going on television sometimes, she always seemed to be going somewhere. Now it was because of a case she'd been working on for a while. She said it was an important one.

But as far as Billy could tell, they all were.

So she was going to be up in Boston for a few days. And his dad was now on the other side of town, even though it already felt to Billy like the other side of the whole country. Billy was ten, and both his parents were always telling him how bright he was. But he wasn't bright enough to figure out what had happened to their family this week.

He wondered sometimes if he was ever going to figure out grown-ups.

His best friend, Lenny, said you had a better chance of figuring out girls.

All he knew for sure, right now, the end of his first official week of living with only one parent in the house, was this: It was about to be no parents in the house. And on this Saturday morning, with his sixteen-year-old sister, Eliza, still at a sleepover and his brother, Ben, already at his piano lesson, pretty soon it would be the quietest house in the world. With their dad gone, at least the arguing between his parents had stopped. Only now Billy couldn't decide what was worse, the arguing or the quiet.

Of course, Peg would be around. Peg: the nanny who had always seemed to be so much more to Billy.

To him, Peg had always been like a mom who came off the bench and into the game every time suitcases were lined up in the hall again and one of the black cars was back in the driveway. It had been that way with Peg even before his dad had up and moved out.

Billy's mom had finished up a call on her cell phone while he finished his breakfast. His dad used to make the pancakes on Saturdays. But his mom had done it today, maybe trying to act like things were normal even if they both knew they weren't.

His mom, whose first name was Lynn, sat down next to him on one of the high chairs they used when they were eating at the counter in the middle of the kitchen.

"Hey, pal," she said.

"Hey."

He speared the last piece of pancake and pushed it through the puddle of syrup on his plate.

"I'm sorry to be leaving so soon, after. . . ." She hesitated, like she would sometimes when Billy would hear her upstairs in her bedroom, practicing one of her courtroom speeches at night.

"After Dad left us," Billy said. "That's what you were going to say, wasn't it?"

"You're right, I was," his mom said. "So soon after that. But you understand it can't be helped, right? I know you don't think your dad and I did a very good job of explaining what's happened to us all. But I hope I explained why I had to go back up to Boston today."

Billy the bright boy said, "Mom, I know it's your job."

"And," Lynn Raynor said, "you understand why I'm having you and Ben and Eliza stay here with Peg and not move over to your dad's place, don't you?"

His mom had already gone over this about ten times. Now Billy was afraid she was going to do it all over again. Maybe it was something lawyers did, explained things until you practically knew them by heart.

"I understand that part, Mom," he said. "This is our home. And you don't want us to get in the habit of going back and forth between you and dad until—"

"Until this whole thing sorts itself out," his mom said, finishing his thought for him.

Billy nodded, even though that was the part he really didn't get, since it seemed to him that things had sorted themselves out already.

They were here.

His dad was there.

Case closed, as his mom liked to say.

"Got it," he said.

"Hey," she said, getting down off her chair. "How about a hug?"

Billy jumped down and gave her one, harder than he'd planned. What she had always called the Big One.

"You be the man of the house while I'm away," she said. "Okay?"

"Okay."

It was the same thing his father had said on Wednesday before he drove away.

But Billy Raynor didn't want to be the man of the house.

He just wanted to be a kid.

TWO

At least it was basketball season.

Billy wasn't the best player on his ten- and eleven-year-old team in the Rec League at the YMCA. Lenny DiNardo was the best player on the Magic, by a lot, even if Billy would never admit that to him. Lenny was one year and one month older than Billy, and seemed to do almost everything better than Billy.

For now, Billy's favorite part about basketball was shooting. His dad was always getting on him to pass more, telling him that there was no law against him passing the ball once in a while, that basketball wasn't one against five, that the last time he'd checked, it was still five against five. But Billy thought of himself as a shooter, one of the best shooters in their league. It wasn't like their team had been losing, so even though he would pass up an open shot sometimes and pass to somebody else, he really didn't think there was anything wrong with the way he played.

His mom would sometimes joke—at least before his dad moved out—that the first thing Billy had inherited from his father was stubbornness.

His dad coached their team. When somebody would ask Joe Raynor what his son's position was, he'd put his hands together like he was getting ready to shoot and say, "*This* position, pretty much."

If Billy was anywhere nearby he'd say, "Funny one there, Dad."

Most of the time, of course, there weren't a lot of laughs around the Magic. His dad was a tough coach, even with Billy. *Especially* with me, Billy thought. "Hard core" was the way his dad would describe his approach to basketball, even Rec League basketball at the Y. He said that was the way he'd been taught to play basketball, and that was the way he was going to teach it.

One time Lenny's dad, a pretty funny guy who didn't seem to take basketball or anything else too seriously, said that it was tough love around Joe Raynor's basketball team, but without much love.

Billy knew his dad loved basketball, and loved him, even though you couldn't tell either one if you were in the gym with them.

Sometimes, Billy thought, his dad seemed happy only when he was talking about how *he* played basketball back when he was the star of their town's high school team. Maybe that was why the first box he'd carried when he moved out had been the one with his trophies and plaques and team pictures in it, the pictures he'd taken down off the wall in his study.

More than anything else, that was what made Billy think his dad was never coming back to live with them. No matter how much "sorting out" both his parents said there was to do.

At least it was basketball season and at least his dad was still his coach, no matter how tough he could be sometimes. And at least there was a game today.

His dad had called on the phone about two minutes after his mom had left for the airport, as if he had some kind of weird radar going that let him know Mom was out of the house. He asked if Billy needed a ride to the Y, but Billy told him that Lenny's mom was picking him up.

"That's okay, right?" Billy said. Not sure these days what was okay and what wasn't.

"Fine," his dad said. "Are you okay, bud?"

"We've got a game, don't we?" Billy said.

"I meant with all this."

Billy, trying to make himself sound older, said, "I guess I'm still kind of sorting this stuff out like everybody else."

There was a pause at his dad's end of the phone, from his house on the other side of town. Then he said, "So how's Ben?"

Ben was nine.

"At piano," Billy said.

"No," his dad said, "I meant how's he doing with me not being around?"

"He's Ben, Dad. You know him. He never says much about anything."

The truth was, Billy, even at ten, wondered if his dad knew his little brother at all. Once they didn't have sports in common, it was as if they didn't have anything in common, except maybe the same last name.

Ben had tried soccer for a couple of years and had been one of the fastest guys on his team. But when it came time to try out for travel soccer, he just quit instead. It was the same with tennis. He had started playing in some clinics at the Racquet Club when he was six, and the few times Billy had watched him, he thought he was one of the better kids his age. Then he had quit tennis. He just didn't care about sports the way their dad did, and the way Billy cared about basketball.

Ben was a piano prodigy.

The only reason Billy even knew what that word meant was because of his brother. Because practically from the time Ben started taking lessons when he was in kindergarten, that's what everybody had been calling him.

Prodigy. "A highly talented child or youth" was what the dictionary said when Billy had looked it up. That was Ben. Like one of those girl tennis players that started beating older players when she was twelve or something.

Ben was so good at playing the piano, right

away, that it was like he never had any choice about doing it. Billy didn't know anything about music and never had any interest in playing any instruments himself, but even he knew when he'd go to one of his brother's piano recitals that what Ben was doing was different from everybody else.

Billy never said this to anybody, not even Lenny, but he wished he were half as good at basketball as Ben was at playing piano.

"Well, tell him I said hi," Joe Raynor said to Billy now on the telephone, "and that maybe I'll stop by after our game."

Billy said he would. When he hung up the phone, he yelled down to where Peg was doing her ironing in the laundry room, told her he was on his way to basketball and that he was going to Lenny's afterward.

He liked being at Lenny's house a lot better these days.

At Lenny's, things were still the way they were supposed to be.

THREE

Once they got on the court, Billy felt better than he had all week.

Maybe Ben felt that way playing the piano today, at his regular Saturday lesson with Mrs. Grace. But being on the court again with Lenny DiNardo and the other Magic players, even going through the drills his dad made them do before every game, made him feel happier than he had since his mom and dad had called them together for the "family conference" after everybody had come home from school on Wednesday afternoon.

From that day on, basketball wasn't just the sport Billy loved the most.

It was the most important thing in his world.

When he was on the court at the Y, catching the ball and feeling the way it settled in his hands right before he put up a shot, that was the only time everything felt right in Billy's world. Even if it was just for a moment.

Billy even liked *practicing* basketball. Sometimes he would hear other guys complaining about having to go to the Magic's one practice a week, on Wednesday nights at West School, like they were being forced to stay after school or something. Billy never felt that way. Practice wasn't as good as playing games. But as far as he was concerned, it was close enough.

The basketball court was Billy Raynor's real home now.

The game was fun today, even though Billy felt a little sad every time he looked up at the clock and saw less time on it. Sometimes when they'd finally get the lead in a close game, he'd want the time to run out.

Not today.

Today they were winning easily against the Mavericks. Billy and Lenny had helped the Magic build a big lead in the first quarter and then sat down in the second quarter and watched their teammates make it even bigger. There were ten players on a team, and the rule at the Y was that every player had to play at least half the game. Some coaches like to split up their very best players, but not Billy's dad. He said that Billy and Lenny were probably going to play together on the high school team someday and might as well learn to play together now. So he'd usually play them in the first quarter and then either the third or the fourth, depending on how the game was going.

Today, Billy knew, it wasn't going to matter when they played in the second half, because the game was going great for them, and nobody on their team seemed to be able to do anything wrong.

Nobody could stop Lenny, and this was one of those days when Billy couldn't miss. Couldn't miss, didn't want to leave. At halftime they were ahead by twenty points.

Billy's dad told Billy and Lenny he was going to play them in the fourth quarter. So they sat and watched in the third quarter as the Mavericks cut the lead a little bit.

The Magic was still ahead by sixteen when

Billy got back in there. And maybe it was because they were winning by so much that he started to goof around a little, try the kind of crazy off-balance shots that only Lenny could make. Billy was shooting even more than he usually did, passing even less than he knew his dad liked, especially with their team ahead by so much.

Billy wasn't trying to show the other team up. There were even a couple of his school friends on the Mavericks. He was just having some fun.

His dad told him to cut it out a couple of times, not yelling or making a big deal out of it. But Billy kept shooting. He'd played about as close to his best as he could today, and after all, he'd just had about the worst week of his whole life.

He figured his dad, more than anybody else, wouldn't mind if he took a few extra shots, especially since most of them were going in.

Only the opposite was happening.

The more he shot, the madder his dad got.

And the madder he got, the madder Billy started to get at him for being mad.

With four minutes left in the game and one of the guys on the Mavericks shooting two free throws,

Lenny whispered to Billy, "What's the deal? You just figure out how steamed you are at him?"

"I'm not," Billy said.

"You sure?" Lenny said.

The next time down the court, Billy came down on a fast break, pulled up and shot from way outside, even though Lenny was wide open, cutting for the basket. The shot missed, but that wasn't what upset his dad.

His dad stood up, yelled at the ref for a timeout, jerked his thumb over his shoulder like he was an umpire throwing a manager out of a baseball game and said to Billy, "Take a seat."

"But I haven't played half the game." It was the only thing Billy could think of to say.

"The way you've been playing the last few minutes," his dad said in a loud voice, "you're lucky I left you in this long."

Billy stood where he was, still a few feet on the court, feeling everybody else in the game and the crowd staring at him, like he was out in the open in paintball.

"We're waiting," his dad said.

Billy looked over at Lenny, standing in front of

their bench, Lenny somehow begging just with his eyes for Billy to get off the court, not make things worse than they already were.

Finally Billy went and sat down as far away from where his dad sat as he could.

Yet when the game started back up, his dad wouldn't drop it. His face was red as he yelled down to Billy, "When you're ready to be part of the group again, you can go back in."

The next thing just came out of Billy, like a button popping off a shirt, even though it was like he was saying it to the floor, his head down.

"What do you know about being part of the group?" he said.

His dad ran to Billy at superhero speed, standing over him, not seeming to care who could hear what they were saying to each other.

"What is that supposed to mean?"

"Nothing," Billy said.

"It didn't sound like nothing to me," his dad said. Still not letting this go. "If you've got something you want to say to me, go ahead and say it," Joe Raynor said.

For one quick second, Billy felt that burn you

get inside your eyes when you think you might start crying, but he put his head down so nobody could see him, squeezed his eyes shut until the feeling went away.

When he was positive he wasn't going to cry, he looked up at his dad. Usually when he was in trouble about something, his dad would have to order Billy to look him in the eyes.

Not today.

"I guess I just need to know something," Billy said. "Are you my coach today or my dad?"

FOUR

They were back at Billy's house in the late afternoon, shooting baskets in the driveway after playing *2006 FIFA World Cup* on Xbox 360 for a couple
of hours at Lenny's.

It was still the middle of winter and pretty
cold, even with the sun out, but Billy and Lenny
didn't care how cold it was. There were times when
they came out here and shot around even when it
was snowing.

Lenny was like a friend and an older brother all
at the same time. Lenny's brother was a *lot* older
than they were, already a sophomore in college. So
it worked out great, almost like they'd planned it
this way. Billy was like the younger brother Lenny

didn't have. Lenny? He was like the older brother Billy sort of wished he had—more than an older sister from Mars.

Billy loved Ben, who in that quiet way of his was one of the coolest people he knew.

He just had more in common with Lenny.

And more fun.

Lenny was saying now, "I didn't know whether your dad was going to ground you for life or just make you run laps forever."

Billy, even with his hands starting to get a little colder now, made another shot from the outside and motioned for Lenny to pass him the ball back.

"Don't worry," Billy said. "I'm not letting him mess up my whole day."

"Just don't let it mess up your whole *season,*" Lenny said. "You know you wait all year for basketball, just like I do."

"I won't, don't worry," Billy said. "We made a deal, remember?"

"Deal?" Lenny said. "You did everything except make me take one of those blood oaths."

Their deal, one they never even talked about

with the other guys on the team, was that they were not just going to win the championship of their age division, they were going to go undefeated.

Billy made another one from outside their three-point line, the one they'd drawn in chalk, the ball hitting nothing but net. The *swish* sound of the ball going through the net reminded him of a big gust of wind.

"Least I can still shoot," Billy said. "Even if somebody acts like I'm the biggest gunner in the world."

"You and your dad just had a bad day," Lenny said.

Like every other day this week, Billy thought.

"You played good the last couple of minutes after he let you back in," Lenny said.

"He must've told you that afterward," Billy said, "because he sure didn't tell me."

"Trust me," Lenny said.

"How do you know?"

"I know things," Lenny said. Then in one of his deep voices, like the cartoon voice of Batman, he said, "Deep and mysterious things."

Lenny knocked the ball out of Billy's hands,

dribbled in, made a reverse layup with his left hand, made that look as easy as eating ice cream.

"And now," Lenny said, "I am going to give you such a good beatdown in one-on-one that you're going to want to take *yourself* out of the game."

"In your dreams," Billy said.

"Shoot for it," Lenny said, flipping him the ball.

"Play till ten baskets?"

"Till dark!" Lenny said.

"If we play winners, it might take you that long just to get on offense," Billy said.

"In *your* dreams," Lenny said.

Billy stepped to their chalk free throw line, drained another shot. "My ball," he said, then handed it to Lenny and said, "Check."

They played one-on-one in Billy's driveway then, played till dark, going after each other the way they always did, shoving and laughing and trash-talking. They hooped it up as hard as they could, so wrapped up in basketball and playing against each other that neither one of them noticed Ben Raynor watching them from his bedroom window, watching them the whole time.

Crying.

FIVE

Once his mom came back from Boston, things started to feel normal.

Not great. Definitely not great.

Just more normal.

It was like a math problem, Billy would think sometimes. The family they used to have, minus one.

One night, after an extra Magic practice, his dad picked up him and Eliza and Ben and took them out for burgers, saying they were going to start doing this at least once a week. Eliza talked even more than she usually did, which was saying something. Even on a slow day she talked so much Billy would stare at her sometimes like she was a science project, waiting to see if she ever actually took a breath.

Sometimes Billy thought that Ben not talking

very much made Eliza think that meant more time for her.

Like it was her job to pick up the slack even more.

The weird part of that night came after dinner, when their dad dropped them off at the house without even coming inside.

"Tell your mom I'll give her a call tomorrow, maybe set something up for the weekend," Joe Raynor said before they got out of the car.

Billy wanted to tell him to come inside and tell her himself—she was just on the other side of the front door—but he didn't.

"Love you guys," his dad said, and Eliza said "Love you, too" for all of them. They walked up the front walk and through the door themselves, Ben coming in last, watching the car until it disappeared around the corner.

Eliza went straight upstairs and in less than a minute, Billy could hear her talking away on her cell phone, probably getting ready to instant-message all her other friends.

"Feel like watching a game with me?" Billy said to Ben.

But Ben shook his head and said he was going to finish watching a movie on his computer, then went upstairs to his own room and shut the door, the way he had pretty much every single night since their dad had left.

Billy poked his head into the dining room, where his mom was working away at her computer, papers spread out all around her on the dining room table.

"Hey," he said.

"Hey, pal, how'd it go?"

"Fine."

"Did your brother eat?"

"Half his burger."

His mom said, "Better than nothing." Then she said, "I'm almost done here." Billy said it was all good, there was a game he wanted to watch.

"When isn't there?" she said, and went back to work.

Billy went into the den, turned on the TV, found the Suns–Cavaliers. It had just started, which meant he could probably watch the whole first half before bed. The first commercial, he snuck into the kitchen and grabbed a bag of Doritos and a small bottle of Gatorade, even though it was way past what his mom called "the junk-food deadline." Then he came back and watched Lenny's man, LeBron, do things with the basketball the announcers said only Michael Jordan had ever done at the same age.

That always annoyed Billy's dad, every time they did that during a Cavs game, because he'd point out that kids like Billy had never even seen Michael Jordan *play*.

This had always been the time of night, the last hour before bed, when Billy and his dad would sit on the couch together in this room and watch games together. His dad would do a better job announcing the game than the real announcers did.

But not tonight.

His dad wasn't there.

Billy had started playing in the Rec League when he was seven. So this was his fourth year playing for his dad, who was the only coach he'd ever had.

Lenny's dad was the assistant coach this year, but he'd only signed on so that Billy and Lenny could play on the same team. Under the rules of the Y, you could play on the team that your dad coached, and each team could have two coaches.

Some dads only coached together so they could put two star players together—it didn't matter to them whether the kids were friends or not. But Joe Raynor and Pete DiNardo had known each other since *they* were kids, and Billy and Lenny were best buds, so the whole thing worked out great for everybody, especially Mr. DiNardo, who only had to come to the games and watch from the bench.

The Magic was Joe Raynor's team, the best one he'd had since he'd started coaching Billy, the best one by far. And he'd made it clear since their very first practice, from the first Wednesday night in the gym at West School, that they were all supposed to have one goal: Win the league championship.

It was something he and Billy had never done together.

They had lost twice in the semifinals, twice in the finals. Last year they were down one point with five seconds left when Billy had gotten fouled and sent to the free throw line to shoot two free throws.

If Billy had made both, his team—known as the
Blue Devils last year—would have been ahead by a
point and probably would have won the game and
the championship of the eight- and nine-year-old
division.

He missed them both.

The first one he shot way too hard, even as he
heard his dad yelling at him to relax from the bench.
It bounced off the backboard and didn't even hit
the rim.

He still had one to tie.

Billy bounced the ball five times like he always
did, because his dad had taught him to always fol-
low a routine when you shot free throws. He took a
deep breath and shot the second one much better,
got that good feeling you get when you think you've
put just the right spin on the ball.

But it was a little too long. The ball caught the
back of the rim and then hit the front of the rim
and hung there, like it couldn't decide whether it
wanted the game to be tied or not, like it was deciding whether the Blue Devils or the Huskies should
win the championship.

It decided on the Huskies.

Billy stared at the rim afterward and felt worse than he ever had about sports, felt the kind of sad that you felt on the last day of summer vacation.

Billy had never forgotten that day, not just because he missed both free throws, but because of the way his dad took the loss, even though he told Billy and everybody else on the Blue Devils how proud he was of them afterward.

He'd told Billy the same thing all the way home, how proud he was of him, how the Blue Devils wouldn't even have been in a position to win the game if Billy hadn't shot the lights out of the basket all day.

But when they did get home, his father had gone into his study, what he called his trophy room—"We're going to add one more to the collection today," he'd said before they left to play the Huskies—and closed the door. He spent the rest of the day behind that closed door, alone.

Now this season, as the Magic had won their first six games, he kept talking to Billy about "unfinished business."

Billy wanted to win the championship this year as much as anybody. More than anything, he wanted to somehow get the chance to make the two free throws he'd missed last year.

It was just that he'd never thought of basketball as any kind of business.

After the Magic won their next game, making it 7–0 for the season, Billy's dad still said he was shooting too much, told him on the way home—Billy's home, not his dad's anymore—that the Magic should have won more easily than they did.

Billy just kept agreeing with him, nodding sometimes, saying "Yes, Dad" sometimes, saying he would keep working on his passing, that he'd do better next week.

Not because he believed what he was saying or actually did think he'd shot too much today. Just because he didn't want this to be another day when he got out of the car feeling like they'd lost instead of won.

"I know I ask a lot of you," his dad said.

You're not kidding, Billy thought.

"I'm asking you to be a big guy in basketball the same way I want you to do that with your brother," his dad said.

"Ben's fine," Billy said. "I think he's just getting himself ready for his big recital."

Billy didn't know when Ben's recital was exactly, just that it was around the time the basketball season ended. Ben had said something one time about how they were both going to be in the playoffs at the same time, just in different things.

"You two ever talk about your mom and me?"

"No."

"I don't talk with him the way I talk with you," his dad said. "But he's good?"

"Dad, he's Ben, okay? You know what Mom thinks about him playing the piano. He lets the piano talk for him."

"I wish sometimes you worked as hard at basketball as Ben does at piano."

They were in front of the house now, the car shut off. That wasn't good.

It meant they weren't done.

"I do work," Billy said. "You see me . . . or used to see me . . . in the driveway."

"I'm talking about working at being a team player." The car wasn't going anywhere, but Billy saw him still gripping the wheel with both hands, hard. "There were a bunch of times today when it should have been pass first with you. But it's always pass last. As in last resort."

Billy felt himself biting his lower lip to keep himself from getting mad. It seemed like it hardly took anything these days for that to happen. Or for his dad to get mad at him.

"That's not true."

"Yes, it is," his dad said. "And I can't let you get away with it. If the coach's son is playing by his own rules, the other guys don't respect him, and they don't respect the coach."

Billy said, "The guys on the team like playing with me."

"You sure about that?"

"You sure they like playing for you?" Billy said.

Sometimes keeping things inside was harder than saying them.

"This isn't about me!" his dad said, his voice sounding so loud in the front seat it was like he'd turned on the radio all of a sudden. Turned it on and turned it up. "This is about being a team, which means everybody being a team player. Starting with you."

"How bad can we be at being team players if we haven't lost a game yet?" Billy said.

"Trust me," his dad said, "we're going to if you don't get with the program."

Billy opened the door on his side now. "I didn't know it was a program," Billy said. "I thought it was just a game."

He ran for the house, ran as fast as he could, like he was in a game of tag and the house was safe.

SIX

When the weather was warm enough, even in the winter, recess at West School was outside, in the period right before lunch. They were outside now on Tuesday morning because it felt like a spring day, even though spring was still more than a few weeks away.

Everybody wanted to go outside even when it was colder than *Ice Age*. When you were in school, you were always looking to get outside, even if it was just for a fire drill.

Billy was in fifth grade at West, Ben was in fourth. Lenny was in sixth, his last year at West before middle school at Hayground. That's the way it worked in their town, you moved up in seventh grade.

They all had the same recess. Billy and Lenny

and their friends had been playing four-square for a while, with lots of stops and starts, mostly because Lenny had rules for four-square that only he could understand.

When they finished, Billy said to Lenny, "Do you think I shoot too much?"

Lenny grinned. "It's pretty much the object of the game in four-square, dude. Keep serving it up."

"You know what I mean."

"Hey," Lenny said. "Everybody in basketball shoots too much sometimes."

"Do you think I shoot a *lot* too much?"

"Nah," he said. "You only do that when you're feelin' it. And when you're feelin' it in hoops, it's like a rule that you gotta keep puttin' it up."

He should have known better than to ask Lenny DiNardo. Lenny was always going to take his side, no matter what. "I've got your back even when you're facing me" was the way Lenny liked to put it.

At least somebody still had his back these days.

It was when they started cutting across the yard to the basketball court after four-square that they saw Zeke Mills, the worst guy in the whole school, pulling Ben Raynor's hoodie over his head and spinning Ben around like they were playing blindman's bluff.

He was known in fifth grade as Zeke the Geek, though never to his face.

His real first name was Zechariah. And he was the biggest bully at West.

Zeke the Geek didn't just terrorize kids in the fifth grade, he did it to kids in *all* the grades.

"C'mon," Billy said to Lenny now, pulling him along, toward where Zeke and Ben were near the playground monkey bars.

"Aw, dude," Lenny said, making "dude" sound like the saddest word in the world, the way he could sometimes. "I want to make it to seventh grade alive."

Billy didn't say anything back because he didn't have time, because he was already running ahead of Lenny. He knew Zeke never needed a good reason to pick on someone. Sometimes all you had to do was make eye contact with him. Or just be one spot ahead of him in the lunch line in the cafeteria.

Billy didn't care why it was happening now, just that it was happening to his brother.

Ben was on the ground when Billy got to him, having fallen over when Zeke spun him around. He was trying in vain to get his head out from under his sweatshirt so he could see.

Billy gave a quick look around, hoping a teacher might be somewhere in the area. But the closest one was Mrs. Ray, back over by the four-square court.

Zeke and the only two friends he had, the Ratner twins, were laughing at Ben as he kept getting more and more tangled in his sweatshirt.

"When you can dress yourself," Zeke said to Ben, "then you can sing us a song."

The Ratner twins started laughing all over again, as if a dumb remark like that was the funniest thing they'd ever heard.

"Ben, it's me," Billy said as he reached down and untangled Ben's hood. "You okay?"

"Yeah," Ben said.

"Why don't you go find your buds?" Billy said,

grabbing him by his arm and pulling him up, the way you did when a guy got knocked down in basketball.

"Hold on, Raynor," Zeke said to Billy. "Not till he sings me a song." Zeke turned to the Ratner twins, whose faces always reminded Billy of pug dogs, and said, "A rap-type song maybe. So's I don't have to rap him again."

All three of them laughed again. Billy had always thought the Ratner twins were dumber than dirt, anyway.

"He doesn't sing, Zeke," Billy said. "He plays the piano. Even you know that."

"Was I talking to you?" Zeke said.

Zeke was looking at Billy like a fly he was about to swat.

"I thought you were," Billy said. "My mistake."

Lenny said, "C'mon, Zeke. This is no biggie. Why don't you just drop it?"

Zeke said to Lenny, "Was I talking to *you*, DiNerdo?"

"Good one, Zeke, no kidding," Billy said. "You've got a real way with words."

It was a miracle, Billy thought, though probably not the kind you heard about in church, that he'd managed to be at West School as long as he had and never officially had a beef with this jerk.

But Billy knew he had one now.

Behind Zeke and the Ratner twins he could see a small crowd forming, though it didn't seem to have attracted the attention of Mrs. Ray or the other teachers in the yard.

The one time he needed a teacher, and he couldn't find one.

With this many kids watching, Billy knew he couldn't back down.

Not even with Zeke the Geek.

"You making fun of me, Raynor?"

"I've got no problem with you, Zeke. I just want you to stop picking on my brother."

"Not until he sings."

"Ben," Billy said, "you go ahead back inside. Recess has gotta be over soon."

"He's not going anywhere," Zeke said.

"Go ahead, Ben."

His kid brother was the nicest person Billy Raynor knew, grown-up or kid, a sweet kid Billy had never seen be mean to anybody. Now Ben looked up at Billy, asking him with his eyes what he should do, really.

Then Ben looked at Zeke.

Still frozen to the spot he'd been standing on since Billy helped him up.

"It's okay," Billy said, in the same voice he'd use when he was showing Ben how to do something new, whether it was a racing dive into their pool in summer or helping him learn to ride a bike when Ben didn't want to wait for their dad to come home from work, running alongside Ben with his hand lightly touching his shoulder.

Ben gave Billy one last look, nodded, put his head down, started to walk away.

Zeke took a fast step, reached out and grabbed him by the arm, then slid his hand down so he had Ben's right hand. The one Billy would watch when Ben played the piano, that hand acting like it had a mind of its own sometimes as it moved back and forth across the keys.

Billy could see from Zeke Mills's face how hard he was squeezing one of his kid brother's piano hands.

Knowing that telling him to stop wasn't going to do any good, Billy stepped forward and chopped down on Zeke's wrist with all his might, like he was trying to pound a nail with his closed fist.

Zeke didn't let go.

Ben wasn't making a sound or begging Zeke to stop. But you could see it on his face, his eyes squeezed shut, how much Zeke was hurting him. Could see the tears starting, somehow coming out of his closed eyes.

Billy did something then he'd never done to another person in his life. He planted himself like he was swinging for the fences in baseball and slugged Zeke the Geek as hard as he could with a punch to his stomach, knocking the wind right out of him.

Now Zeke let go, falling backward as he did, his face the color of the red jacket he was wearing, trying to catch his breath.

But Billy knew a couple of things. One, Zeke wasn't going to be out of breath for long.

Here was the other:

Whatever happened next wasn't going to be good.

In the distance he could hear a woman, probably Mrs. Ray, yelling for them to stop.

"Zeke," Billy said, "I'm not looking to fight with you."

"You should've thought of that before, Raynor."

Zeke charged him then.

Billy didn't know whether he planned to tackle him or punch him or both, but decided he couldn't wait to find out. So he closed his eyes, got down as low as he could, got his arms around him like it was a game of tackle football in the yard.

And was the most surprised kid at West School when both of them went down.

SEVEN

They both got suspended.

Lenny told Mrs. Marion, the school principal, what he'd seen. So did Ben. But so many other kids at West School were afraid of Zeke Mills they all said what he told them to say, which was that Billy was the one who started it.

Mrs. Marion said she didn't really care who started it, that fighting was never an option at her school, and that both Billy and Zeke were getting suspended for the rest of today and all of tomorrow.

When his father got to school—Mom, as it turned out, was on a big conference call at her office—Billy had to sit there while Mrs. Marion told both versions of the fight. First Billy's, then Zeke's. When she was finished, Joe Raynor told her that she had no choice but to suspend him, even if Billy was defending his brother, and that something like this would never happen again, she could count on that.

When they got in the car, Billy said to his dad, "Do you even care what really happened?"

"Ben already told me," his father said.

"You're saying I shouldn't have stuck up for him?"

"I'm saying that there's better ways to handle stuff like this than fighting in the middle of recess."

"You weren't there," Billy said.

He pictured Zeke squeezing Ben's hand again, pictured Ben starting to cry, wondered if Ben had told his dad that Zeke had made him cry.

Just because no guy ever wanted to admit that, especially to his dad.

"Did Ben even tell you—"

"Tell me what? That you weren't thinking? That you don't know actions have consequences?"

"Never mind," Billy said.

"Even in the school yard," his dad said, "when you want to take a shot, you do."

Then he told Billy he wasn't allowed to practice with the Magic the next night. And on Joe Raynor's teams, everybody knew the rule: If you didn't practice—unless you were sick—you didn't get to play the next game.

"It's not fair," Billy said when his mom got home and he had told her his side of things.

"Getting suspended from school," she asked, "or having to miss the game on Saturday?"

"Both," he said.

"I know," she said. "You ended up getting socked twice."

"So you agree with me," he said.

"Not about the fighting," she said. "Even if you were sticking up for Ben."

He was under the covers. She was sitting at the end of his bed, the way she still did sometimes, though not as often as she had before she got this busy.

"Mom," Billy said, sitting up now, his back against the headboard, "that jerk was hurting Ben's hand. I couldn't let somebody do that, even if it was Zeke the Geek."

"I'm glad you were there," she said. "I know Ben was glad you were there. But the law's the law. Isn't there some rule in basketball that if you even try to throw a punch, you get suspended for a game?"

"The NBA," Billy said, then he said, "Wait, you know that?"

"I was . . . I'm married to your father," she said. "I had to pick up a few sports things along the way."

"Why is Dad acting like this?" Billy said. "It's like nothing I do is right anymore."

She said, "Your father likes order in his life. You know that about him, right? Like his tools in the garage, everything in its place."

"Now stuff is out of place."

"Big-time," his mom said.

"But I'm not the one who left," Billy said. "He did."

"One more thing that's out of order," she said. "Like we say in court."

She reached forward and took his hand, rubbed his arm the way she used to when he was little and she wanted to help him get to sleep.

Billy let her.

"I'm sorry I messed up, Mom," Billy said. "At school, I mean."

"Sometimes we all do that," she said. "Even with the best of intentions." She winked at him and said, "How come you think lawyers like me stay so busy?"

"Maybe I needed a lawyer," Billy said.

She smiled. He smiled. Sometimes Billy felt like he'd been missing his mom even more than his dad, even though she was the parent still living in the house.

His dad called on Saturday morning and said Billy could come to the game if he wanted to, support the team from the bench, be sort of like an assistant coach. Billy thought it might be some kind of Dad test, maybe a way for him to prove that he could somehow be a better team player by *not* playing.

Billy didn't care, not today.

He knew that as much as it was going to kill him to miss the game, it would be much worse having to sit there at the Y and watch. And he still thought it was wrong that he wasn't getting to play against the Nuggets, who weren't one of the better teams in their league but who were good enough to beat the Magic with him out of the lineup.

He told his dad on the phone that he didn't feel like it, he was going to stay home and work on some stuff he needed to work on, which was technically true, even though in his mind he was only talking about Xbox 360 and *NCAA Live*.

"Your call," his dad said.

"Yup."

"I'd like to have you there as my assistant coach," his dad said.

"Would you?" Billy said, not even caring if it came out sarcastic. Then he said he had to go, that Mom was calling him.

It was him, Ben, Eliza, Mom and Peg for breakfast. Peg was cooking up one of her specialties, even though she called just about everything she cooked one of her specialties. Today it was waffles. Somehow when Peg made them, they came out of the waffle iron bigger and fatter than anybody else's.

Eliza had been talking about some party for the high school basketball team she'd been to the night before, as if anybody else at the table besides Mom cared. Billy stopped listening about the time she said the captain of the team had given her and her friend Maggie rides home. Billy was thinking about his *own* team, about the gym and the Y on Saturday mornings, how the best part of his whole week was walking through those double doors, usually seeing another game ending when he got inside, hearing the whistles and the cheers of the parents and coaches and the horn sounding when somebody would make a sub.

He could practically hear all that sitting at his own kitchen table better than he could hear what his own sister was saying.

He just wanted it to be eleven o'clock, when he knew the game would be over.

Eliza's cell phone started playing whatever new annoying song she had on it. The phone, as usual, was on the table next to her plate. She grabbed it right away, checked to see the number that was calling her like she always did, then put it right to her ear and said, "Tell me everything he said after he dropped me off."

"Well," Lynn Raynor said, watching Eliza disappear toward the living room, "this has been more restful than breakfast in bed."

Peg was bringing Billy and Ben seconds. As she put the new waffles on their plates, she said, "Don't worry, boys, you'll get to talk when Liza's in college."

Billy's mom smiled. "Are you sure, Peg? I love my daughter to death, but I picture her still talking to us on speaker phone."

Not even worrying that Eliza might hear, just because Peg could say pretty much anything she wanted and get away with it, Peg said, "That girl can talk the way birds in the morning can sing."

Billy had no idea how old Peg was. She wouldn't tell and neither would his mom. She had curly hair that seemed to be somewhere between red and brown, a round face, the same round glasses she'd always worn. To Billy, it was like she had stayed the same age from the first time he remembered her being around.

And he couldn't remember a time in his life when she wasn't around.

"Ben Raynor," she said, "you eat up now. You need to get to piano."

His mouth full of waffles, Ben said something that Billy was pretty sure was "Yes, Peg."

Peg said, "Then get busy with that toothbrush of yours, which felt drier than *dirt* to me this morning."

Ben mumbled out an answer that seemed to include "brushed."

"We *know* you brushed, Benjamin Raynor," Peg said. "Question is, when?"

Ben swallowed the rest of his waffle and smiled at her then.

"You know I brushed," he said.

"I do," Peg said, smiling back. "But I got to test you now and then."

When nobody else in the family could get a smile out of him, Peg could, even when she was busting him the way she was right now.

"Billy," his mom said, "are you sure you don't want to go to the game? I could drop you on my way to the office."

He wasn't even surprised anymore when she worked on a Saturday. His mom told him all the time how she had worked seven days a week to get herself a scholarship to Harvard and then worked even harder than that to put herself through Harvard Law, which made Billy wonder if they had somehow added days of the week when she was in law school.

Lately she liked to say that she wasn't going to stop working now, with the finish line in sight.

Even though she never really explained where the finish line was.

She kissed Billy and Ben, saying Eliza would be heading over to Maggie's later for a sleepover and that she'd be home from work in time to take Billy and Ben out for burgers at The 1770 House, which they all knew was the best burger in town.

"Last chance on the game," she said at the back door. "Going once, going twice—"

Billy looked at her and said, "Mom, I don't want to see Dad today."

His mom started to say something but didn't, just came back across the room, leaned down and hugged him. Then she was out the door, calling over her shoulder that it was pretty cold out today and Peg could drive Ben to piano, even though Mrs.

Grace, his piano teacher, only lived two blocks away. And it wasn't really two blocks if Ben cut through some backyards.

"I want to walk," Ben said.

"It's no bother, little guy," Peg said.

"I'm *not* little!" Ben said. "I'm nine years old!"

Peg went over and put a hand on his shoulder. As soon as she did, it was like she'd thrown some kind of switch and Ben wasn't mad anymore.

"My bad, big boy," she said. "You're not only nine, you're a lot older than that some of the time. Now eat up so you won't be late for your lesson. We're moving up on that recital of yours. After that, look out, Carnegie Hall."

Peg was from Brooklyn, New York City, and had explained to them that Carnegie Hall was this place in New York where the best piano players in the whole world got to play.

Billy and Ben finished their breakfast without either one of them talking. With Eliza gone, the kitchen seemed as quiet as the school library. It was like that a lot, Billy feeling as if he and Ben were alone, even when they were in a room together. He was thinking about the game he was missing, getting ready to start in about a half hour. Maybe Ben was thinking about piano.

Most of the time, Billy had no idea what his brother, who could be harder to read than a schoolbook, was thinking.

When Ben was gone, Billy went into the den, what had been his dad's room, and started to play *NCAA Live,* which Lenny had left there the day before, knowing he was coming back over after the game. Peg said she was going downstairs to catch up on her ironing, though Billy wondered how there was ever anything to catch up on. She seemed to be down in the basement, listening to her music and ironing, about half the day.

Billy got into his video game as much as he could, telling himself that fake basketball would have to do today, until the game at the Y was over and Lenny was calling with the final score, as he'd promised he would.

He played until the phone rang, knowing he had to get it, that there was no chance of Peg even hearing it from downstairs, not with the way she kept her old-fashioned music cranked up on the speakers they'd all chipped in and got her for Christmas, the ones that went with her new iPod.

Billy ran into the kitchen, but his mom must have left the receiver somewhere when she was walking around talking on it before, and Billy couldn't spot it anywhere. And he knew that by the time he got to the phone upstairs it would be too late, the answering machine would already have picked up.

So he just stood there, feeling helpless, while he heard his mom's voice on the tape saying they couldn't come to the phone right now, to please leave a message and they'd get back to whoever it was.

He looked at the clock over the sink. It was a couple of minutes before eleven. Maybe the game had ended early.

Only the voice on the machine wasn't Lenny's.

It belonged to a woman.

"This is Charlotte Grace," the voice said. "I was wondering why Ben didn't show up for piano this morning."

EIGHT

Before Billy could even worry about where Ben was or what could have happened to him on the way to Mrs. Grace's house, whether he should go tell Peg or call his mom at work, his brother came walking into the kitchen with his hoodie on, acting like everything was completely normal, giving Billy his normal greeting.

"What up?" Ben said.

"Hey," Billy said.

"What've you been doing?" Ben said.

"Playing video."

"Cool."

Billy said to his brother, "How was piano?"

Ben grabbed a small bottle of red Gatorade out of the refrigerator, then walked out of the kitchen saying, "The usual."

Billy heard Ben go up the stairs, then heard his door shut. He was still standing by the small table that the phone was on, the one with the message machine attached to it.

The light was blinking because of Mrs. Grace's message.

Billy stared at it for what felt to him like an hour and finally hit the button that erased it.

Then he headed for the stairs, thinking this was one time when his little brother was going to have to talk.

Ben's room was neat. *Really* neat.

He had his piano trophies lined up in neat rows on the top shelves built into the wall next to his desk. The few trophies he'd gotten in soccer and tennis—Billy knew by now that all you basically had to do was show up in sports to get some kind of trophy—were on one of the bookshelves on the other side of the desk, next to the window looking out over where Billy's hoop was at the end of the driveway.

Everything here seemed to have an assigned

place, like an assigned seat in class. His bed was made, without Peg or their mom having made it. The top of his desk was clear of everything except his laptop. When Billy opened the door and then closed it behind him, he even noticed that Ben's hoodie was hanging on a hook.

Basically his brother's room always looked as if Peg had just finished cleaning up. Except that when she went in there, she hardly had anything to do.

Billy's room was another story.

When she walked into Billy's room, with stuff all over his bed and all over the floor, and his desk so messy you almost couldn't see his laptop, Peg would put her hands on her hips and give him a look and say, "You think whoever got in here found what they were looking for?"

Billy knew what he was looking for when he came into Ben's neat bedroom:

The truth.

He had never known his brother to lie to him, about anything.

Until now.

Ben was on his bed, headphones on, listening to his iPod. He didn't notice Billy at first, but when he did, he took off his headphones and said, "You need something?"

"I just wanted to make sure piano went okay," Billy said, turning around the chair at Ben's desk and sitting down in it.

"You already asked me that downstairs."

"Just double-checking," Billy said. "You know how they're always telling me I've got to be the man of the house now."

"So," Ben said, "you're doing that by double-checking about a piano lesson you've never asked me about before?"

Even though Ben was younger, he always sounded like the older one when they were talking, almost like he was the big brother.

"Something like that."

He didn't know why it was suddenly so important to him that Ben come out with it on his own, come right out and say that he'd lied about going to Mrs. Grace's and was lying about it now.

But it was important.

He said, "Anything else you want to tell me?"

"Nope. Like I told you, it was just the usual."

He was starting to adjust his headphones when Billy said, "Do you think it's usual that Mrs. Grace just called and said you didn't show up for your lesson today?"

Ben, being neat about things even now, took his headphones off, wrapped the cord around the middle, set them on the headboard of his bed, placing the iPod right next to them. "Mrs. Grace called?" he said.

"I just said that."

Ben looked down at his piano hands, and now he didn't say anything.

"You're busted, dude. You lied, and you never lie."

Ben didn't even try to deny it now, just looked at him, eyes big, and said, "Are you going to tell Mom?"

"I'm not Eliza," Billy said. "I don't tell on people."

"Promise?"

"Yeah," Billy said. "On one condition."

"You want me to clean your room for a week, I'll do it, I swear," Ben said. "Just tell me."

"No," Billy said. "*You* tell *me* why you blew off piano and didn't tell anybody."

"I didn't feel like it, is all."

"You love piano."

"Why? Because I'm supposed to be so good at it?" Ben said, the words sounding loud and mad at the same time.

He didn't sound anything like Ben.

"I just know—"

"You *don't* know!" Ben said. Billy could see the piano hands balled up into fists, like Ben was the one who wanted to punch something now. Or somebody. "You're like everybody else in our house. The ones who're still here, anyway. You all just know what you *think* you know."

Billy had come in here thinking he was going to get in Ben's face. Only now Ben had somehow turned the whole thing around.

It was Billy who was on the defensive.

"You—you've got your recital coming up," he said.

"So what?" Ben said. "It's just another stupid recital."

"But you've worked your butt off the whole year," Billy said.

"So that means I can take one stupid Saturday off, right?"

"Is that all it's been? One day off?"

There was a look on Ben's face like he wanted to say something, but then he must have changed his mind. Like in a game, deciding to pass instead of shoot. "Leave me alone," he said.

Billy stood up, not knowing what to say to that.

Ben said, "Are you really not going to tell?"

"If I say I'm not, I'm not," Billy said. "I erased the message."

"Then could you *really,* please, leave my room now?" Ben said.

"What," Billy said, "it was all right to have me around when Zeke the Geek was going to beat on you, but now you want to blow me off?"

It was like everything that was making him mad, including Ben lying, came pouring out of him all at once. Somehow he was as mad at his brother as he'd been at Zeke.

Before Ben could say another word, Billy shouted at him, "I've got enough things to worry about right now without worrying about you, too!"

Billy left, slamming the door behind him, out of breath like he'd been running, thinking: Things are getting more weird around here by the day.

NINE

At basketball practice the next Wednesday, Billy's dad tried to act as if nothing had happened, as if there'd been no fight with Zeke, as if Billy hadn't missed the last practice.

As if he hadn't missed the last game.

The Magic, Billy knew by now, had ended up beating the Nuggets by two points. Those points came on a put-back basket by Lenny with what the rest of the players on the team said was one second left and Lenny said was more like three or four, telling Billy it was hard to know because the other team was out of time-outs, and just took the ball in after Lenny's hoop and threw it down the court.

Lenny was somebody who really never lied, especially about basketball.

"Everybody keeps making a big deal out of it,"

Lenny said to Billy before practice started. "But my guy didn't box me out, and then the ball came right to me, dog. If I'd missed a chippy like that, I should be playing hockey or something."

Peg had brought them, so they were there early. Peg always got you everywhere early, whether it was school or the movies or basketball practice. Peg time, she called it. Billy's dad was the same way. He showed up five minutes before five, the way he always did, went and sat in the folding chair the janitor at West School always left for him on Wednesdays and started writing out what he wanted to do at practice today.

Sometimes Billy wondered if college or pro coaches were as organized with their teams as Joe Raynor was in the Rec League at the Y.

But other than some of those college coaches he watched on TV, the ones whose heads Billy thought might explode at any second, he believed that most of them probably smiled more than his dad.

As usual, they worked on one specific thing for the first part of practice, before they got to do what they really wanted to do—scrimmage. Today, Billy's dad said they were going back to basics on the way he wanted them to start their fast break:

The big guys making a good outlet pass to one of the guards out on the wing, the ball going to the middle from there, everybody filling a lane after that.

When they were at the other end of the court, far enough away so Billy's dad couldn't hear, Lenny said that he was pretty sure even guys in the Highway Patrol didn't worry as much about people being in the right lanes as their coach did.

They ran the fast break drill for about fifteen minutes and Billy didn't hear a thing from his dad, didn't hear his name called one time, until he messed up a couple of times right at the end. On the last one he was slow getting to the middle. Lenny whipped the ball to where Billy was supposed to be, and it went bouncing off the court and up into the first row of bleachers.

Billy's dad blew his whistle and then they heard the one word they hated to hear when they thought any boring drill was about to be over.

"Freeze."

Like cops yelled at guys on cop shows.

Billy stayed where he was, nowhere near the middle of the court.

His dad was in the middle of the court, saying to him now, "Hey, Billy." Maybe to everybody else it came out sounding nice and friendly. Billy knew better. This was the sarcastic tone of voice he hated from his dad. "Can you guess where I am right now?"

Looking down, as if he were talking to his sneaks, Billy said, "In the right spot?"

Smiling but not meaning it, his dad said, "Actually, I'm Billy Raynor doing something the right *way*. Even if it's not something as exciting as shooting. If I'm here, that means I'm Billy Raynor and I'm focusing, even though I'm bored."

"I'm not bored," Billy said. "And I have been focusing. I just messed up."

"If you were focusing," his dad said, "you would've been here when I froze everybody, and I'd be over there. Isn't that right?"

Give it up, Billy told himself.

It was the only way this stuff ever ended. No matter how stubborn he could get, nobody could beat his dad when it came to being stubborn.

You had a better chance beating him at arm wrestling.

"Yes, sir," he said.

"I thought so."

Billy told himself he wasn't going to get the Big Whistle, or get singled out, one time while they scrimmaged, and he didn't. The only shots he took were layups, all but one of them coming on a feed from Lenny.

Most of the time, he was the one feeding Lenny today. When they would run one of his dad's beloved plays, Billy would run it all the way through, going from spot to spot like it was one of those connect-the-dots pictures you drew when you were little. Sometimes when they were setting up one of the plays, he'd move one of the other guys if they weren't in the right place.

His man, Danny Timms, didn't score a single point.

Right after Billy's dad yelled out that next basket ended it, Billy faked what would have been his first outside shot, pulled the ball down, passed it to a wide-open Jim Sarni, who got one last layup for their team.

They all got the Big Whistle now, but they knew it just meant practice was over for today.

Billy thought for sure his dad would at least say something about the pass, since that seemed to be the only thing he cared about these days.

"Good job today, guys," he said, before telling them all he'd see them Saturday.

Good job today, *guys*.

Not the guy who was his own son.

Billy held out some hope, though not a whole lot, that his dad might say something about the way he'd scrimmaged today on the way home, since it was his day to drive.

But when Joe pulled up in front of the house that used to be his house, and Billy and Lenny both got out because Lenny was staying for dinner, he just said the same thing he'd said at the end of practice.

"Good job today, guys," he said. "See you Saturday."

Can hardly wait, Billy thought.

TEN

The next Saturday Ben skipped piano again.

He didn't make anything up this time or act like he was going, when all he planned to do was walk around for an hour. He simply told Peg he was sick to his stomach and was going back to bed.

It was Peg he told because their mom was up in Boston working. There weren't any weekends for his mom.

Peg said, "It can't be something you ate, since you ate like a bird at dinner last night and you haven't hardly touched your eggs this morning."

Ben made the kind of face you did when you smelled *rotten* eggs. "I don't know what it is," he said. "But even talking about food makes me want to throw up."

Eliza, eating her own breakfast with a copy of

Lucky magazine in front of her, didn't even look up. "Gross," she said.

"Ben Raynor," Peg said with hands on her hips, which always meant business. "Are you telling me the truth, or are you looking for a reason to get out of piano today?"

Ben gave a quick look at Billy, then said to Peg, "I don't lie."

"You never have," Peg said. "I'll call Mrs. Grace and tell her."

Ben shot up out of his chair and said, "It's my lesson. I should be the one to call." He went across the room and took the phone out of its holder and started punching in numbers as he walked through the door that led into the dining room. In a few seconds, they heard him talking in a low voice.

Peg said to Billy and Eliza, "That boy isn't himself lately."

"No one around here is," Eliza said. "Except me, of course." She turned a page in her magazine and said, "I *so* have to have that purse."

Ben came back in, put the phone back in its place and said, "I told her I'd see her next Saturday."

To Billy he said, "Good luck with your game," and then headed up the back stairs to his room.

The Magic were playing the Hornets, the only other undefeated team in the league, in the last game for both teams before the play-offs started next Saturday. If everything went the way Billy and Lenny thought it would after that, the next time they'd see the Hornets after today would be at the championship game in two weeks.

Basically, all today's game was supposed to do was decide which team would be the number-one seed going into the play-offs and which team would be number two, but Billy knew better.

He knew that this game was going to feel like the championship of something, even if it was just the championship of today.

When the doorbell rang, Peg looked up at the clock and said to Billy, "I thought Lenny wasn't coming for another twenty minutes?"

"He must be operating on Peg time today," Billy said.

And he knew why. Lenny couldn't wait to get to the Y, either.

When Billy opened the front door, he saw that

Lenny wasn't wearing a jacket or coat or hoodie, just his Magic jersey and shorts, despite the cold. Cold didn't bother Lenny DiNardo because hardly anything did. "I know I'm early," he said. "But, well, you know."

"I know," Billy said.

He started to close the door behind them, then stopped, saying to Lenny, "Give me one sec, I forgot something upstairs."

He ran back up the stairs. Ben's door was shut, as usual. Billy knocked, didn't wait—as usual—before poking his head in.

"What up?" Ben said.

"Just wanted to tell you I'm out of here," Billy said. "And check you out one more time before I left."

Ben said, "I just don't feel good."

"You seemed fine when you got up," Billy said. "I'm just saying."

"I was faking," Ben said, quickly adding, "when I got up, I mean."

Billy said, "Or you're faking now."

Ben turned over on his bed, so he was facing away from Billy. "Go play your game, okay?"

"Not before I find out what's really wrong with you," Billy said.

"You think I'm blowing off piano again, don't you?" Ben said.

"Are you?"

Ben didn't say anything right away. Didn't turn around. Billy didn't know what to say, either. He knew he was the older brother here, by a year. Yet he never felt a year smarter around Ben.

He'd always thought Ben was the smart one of the kids in the family, as if he was the one who had the most of their mom in him.

Billy wanted to be smart enough to get something out of him now, as much as he wanted to get out to the car and get to the game.

The best he could do, still talking to the back of his brother's head, was this:

"Well, any time you want to talk."

"I don't," Ben said. "Have a good game."

He headed back down the front stairs. From the kitchen, he could hear Eliza, either talking to Peg or on the phone.

They all made fun of her and how the only thing she seemed to love more than purses or clothes or shoes or music or instant messaging was the sound of her own voice. But the way Ben was acting lately, Billy didn't mind that sound so much these days.

At least when Eliza was around, somebody in the house actually seemed happy.

He found out in the car that his dad wasn't coming to the game.

His dad never missed a practice or a game. But as soon as Billy did everything but dive into the backseat, apologizing for keeping them waiting, Mr. DiNardo said that he'd just gotten a call on his cell. Billy's dad, he said, had some big emergency with his biggest client and had to go straight to his office.

Now neither one of his parents was having a weekend this weekend, Billy thought.

"So I guess you guys are stuck with me today," Mr. DiNardo said.

Billy and Lenny didn't act as if they were stuck with anybody. They pretty much reacted the way you did when you walked into the classroom and saw an easy substitute teacher you'd had before, one who will let you do pretty much whatever you want to, short of having a spitball war.

"High five," Lenny said.

Billy gave him one that produced a loud slap.

"Bump," Lenny said.

They bumped fists.

Mr. DiNardo, a funny guy who was the morning disc jockey on the town radio station, was checking them both out in the rearview mirror while they were stopped at a red light on Cherry Street. He said, "For a game this big, you guys have a lot of confidence in me."

Lenny looked at his dad in the rearview mirror. The two of them looked exactly alike to Billy, and now they had the same grin on their faces.

Just like that, Billy couldn't believe how jealous he felt, just looking from one face to the other, seeing again how much the two of them liked each other. Trying to remember the last time it was as easy being with his dad as it was for Lenny to be with Mr. D.

Sometimes Billy wished he and his dad could like each other as much as they said they loved each other.

"It's not exactly you we're confident about, Pop," Lenny said. "It's *us*."

"Hold on to that thought," Mr. D said. "Because you guys both know I'm a basketball coach in name only."

"Don't worry, Mr D," Billy said, feeling as cocky as his friend Lenny all of a sudden. "We got you today."

He wasn't sure whether he was really feeling cocky, or whether he was just happy that he was going to get to play ball today without his dad looking over his shoulder.

Maybe he was just happy for once to be playing for somebody else's dad.

ELEVEN

They were ahead almost the whole game.

Never by more than ten points. It wasn't like they were running away with anything, not against the Hornets. Not against Tim Sullivan, the guy Billy considered the second-best player in the league after Lenny.

Tim Sullivan was taller than Lenny, tall enough to play forward in their league, or even center if he wanted. But in his case, size didn't matter. Tim Sullivan was a point guard, had always been a point guard, and the only other point guard who could come close to covering him, because of how big he was and how good he was, was Lenny DiNardo.

Tim Sullivan was the player Billy's dad was always talking to him about. He said Billy should be more like him, that even though Tim could get his shot against any player in the league or any defense, even though he seemed to always have the ball in his hands when he was in the game, he managed to keep everybody else on his team "involved."

That was a big word with Billy's dad.

Involved.

He made it sound like something you did in church instead of a gym.

Today, though, as much as Tim was keeping his teammates involved, the Magic were winning the game. In Billy's mind, there were two big reasons for that:

1) Lenny *was* doing a good job guarding Tim.

2) Billy Raynor couldn't miss.

Could. Not. Miss.

He felt the way he did sometimes at the Pop-A-Shot they had in the basement, when he'd be down there by himself and get a good rhythm going. He'd make everything he threw at the basket until the clock ran out.

That kind of day.

Mr. DiNardo wasn't telling him he was shooting too much because nobody was. If anything, the guys on his team wanted him to shoot *more*.

So he had that going for him. And this: Because the Magic were down a couple of players, he and Lenny got to play the whole second half.

"That's the way your dad would do it, right?" Mr. DiNardo said at halftime.

Billy and Lenny answered at the same time. "Abso*lutely,* Coach," they said.

"I think that's the first time anybody ever called me Coach," Mr. D said.

The Hornets tried to switch from zone to man-to-man in the third quarter. They even switched Tim Sullivan over to Billy. It made Billy mad the first couple of times down the court, Tim guarding him so closely, ignoring everybody else, that Lenny couldn't get him the ball.

Guarding him so tight those first couple of times Billy could hardly breathe.

Lenny could see how annoyed Billy was. When Tim was shooting a couple of free throws, he came over and stood next to him. "Dude," he said, "they had to put the big dog on you. It's a compliment."

The switch actually worked for the Magic, because Lenny started scoring anytime he wanted to against Tony Gilroy, the guy from the Hornets who was guarding him now. After about two minutes, the Hornets had to switch back, Tim going back on Lenny. Before the quarter ended, Billy hit two straight shots, and the Magic were back to being ahead by ten.

It looked like they would stay ahead, not let the Hornets get any closer than that, until Lenny picked up his fourth foul with six minutes left. He called the time-out before his dad did and took himself out of the game.

As he was leaving the court, he said to Billy, "Don't let the other guys panic if they make a run. 'Cause they probably will make one now, without me in there."

"No worries, dude," Billy said, trying to sound more confident than he felt. Because sometimes when Lenny wasn't out there with him, he felt as if he were trying to play with only one sneaker on.

The Hornets made their run, just like Lenny said they would. They scored three baskets in a row in the first minute Lenny was on the bench, then even when Lenny put himself back in, they scored two more baskets on turnovers.

Just like that, the game was tied.

This was a whole different game from the one they'd been playing all morning.

It stayed tied into the last two minutes. The Hornets stayed in their man-to-man, Tim on Lenny, Tony Gilroy on Billy. Billy hit another one on the outside, snuck away on a fast break, getting to the middle just like his dad would have wanted. He wasn't sure, but keeping track inside his head, he had twenty points now, the most he'd ever scored in a game.

He knew it would make his dad crazy if he even thought Billy was keeping track of his own points.

But his dad wasn't here.

The game was still tied with twenty seconds left.

Lenny called their last time-out. Everybody knew he was the one who'd really been coaching the team all game long. He wasn't going to stop now. In the huddle he told everybody where they should go on the last play, what they should do. The rest of the guys out there with him—Billy, Jeff Wilpon, Jim Sarni, Danny Timms—just listened.

When Lenny was finished, he looked up at his dad, as if remembering he was still there, and said, "If that's okay with you, of course, Dad."

Mr. DiNardo smiled.

"Boys," he said, "you just do exactly what my son the coach told you to do."

There was nothing tricky about the play Lenny had come up with. He said there was no way he could take Tim Sullivan one-on-one. But he wanted Tim to think he was going to try, anyway. He was going to drive to his right like he wanted to go around him on the baseline, have Jim Sarni set pretty much what would be a fake screen on him.

At the same time he was making his move, he wanted Jeff Wilpon to run over to the other side of the court and set a pick for Billy.

The way Lenny said it would happen from there, Billy would cut around Jeff's pick, then be open when Lenny passed him the ball a couple of steps inside the free throw line.

Everybody knew it was Billy's favorite spot.

And *then*, if everything had gone the way it was supposed to, Billy would make one more open shot today and the Magic would be the number-one seed going into the play-offs.

And they would still be undefeated.

Lenny made his move with ten seconds left. Jim set his pick on Tim, Lenny took a couple of more dribbles to his right like he was going hard down the baseline.

Only he put the brakes on.

Tony Gilroy, Billy's man, turned to watch. As he did, Jeff came over and set a pick on *him*.

Billy blew past both of them, busting it the way Lenny had told him to, and headed toward the lane.

One small problem: Tim Sullivan was running at him from his right almost at the exact same moment Lenny was getting ready to pass Billy the ball. Billy thought about cutting the other way, toward the basket. But when he gave a quick look behind him, he saw Tony Gilroy scrambling back into the play, coming hard from Billy's left.

There was still plenty of time to give the ball right back to Lenny, who Billy could see was wide open now.

But Lenny, who usually would take the last shot himself, had wanted Billy to do it this time, or he wouldn't have drawn up this play in the huddle. And Billy wanted in the worst way to be the kind of guy who had the ball in his hands in moments like this, who wasn't afraid to take the last shot in a game, no matter how hard a shot it was.

Hero shots, Lenny called them.

Making one against somebody as good as Tim Sullivan was going to make it all that sweeter.

He knew he wasn't passing the ball now, passing up a chance like this.

Billy squeezed between Tim and Tony instead, leaned in the way he thought only Lenny could for one of his hero-shot moves, took one last dribble and let the ball go.

The shot was still in the air when the horn went off.

Billy had stumbled right after he shot, tripping over Tony Gilroy's leg, ended up sitting pretty much under the basket as regulation ended between the Magic and the Hornets.

It ended this way:

With his shot hitting nothing but net.

Magic 42, Hornets 40.

The Magic were still the only undefeated team in the league.

Lenny got to Billy first, then Jim, then Jeff, then Danny Timms and the rest of the guys. Mr. D came next, saying, "Okay, you guys are 10–0 but, hey, I'm 1–0." He grinned at Billy then, looking more like Lenny than ever, and gave him some fist to bump.

It was when Mr. D stepped away to hug Lenny that Billy saw his dad standing in the corner of the gym, almost hidden by the end of the bleachers, arms crossed, not looking happy, not looking sad.

Just there.

Watching everything that was happening around the Magic's basket.

Billy walked over to him. Maybe somebody else would have gone running after a game like this, jumped right up into his dad's arms.

But it wasn't like that with them.

Billy walked.

"You were here?" he said.

"Got here with about eight minutes left to play," his dad said. "When it still looked like we were going to win easy."

"How come you didn't coach?"

"It was Pete's game to win or lose," he said. Pete was Mr. DiNardo. "You don't just show up and tell him to move over. That's not the way it works in sports."

Billy wanted to get back with the guys, get back to the celebration. But before he left, he had to ask.

"What did you think of that last shot?" he said.

His dad didn't even hesitate.

"Lenny didn't have a guy within ten feet of him," he said. "You should've passed."

TWELVE

"Yo," Lenny said at recess on Monday. "I still can't believe your dad dogged you that way after we won the game."

"Me, neither," Billy said.

"Sounded to me like more of that tough love my dad is always joking about," Lenny said. He used his fingers to put little brackets around *tough love* the way Eliza would sometimes.

"Yeah," Billy said. "Except the joke was about as funny as the Ratner twins."

"The Ratner twins are funny," Lenny said. "Just not the way those two dopes think."

They were sitting on a couple of swings that had been on the playground at West from the time when it was one of the lower schools in town. The daily four-square game was still going on, but Billy and Lenny had bagged out of it, saying they were giving everybody else a chance today.

"Not only did you make the winning shot," Lenny said. "You made it against Tim Stinking Sullivan."

"You noticed, huh?" Billy said. "Least somebody did."

"He just thinks he's toughening you up, or whatever, for the play-offs," Lenny said. He was tossing some small, smooth rocks he'd picked up into a plastic trash can about ten yards away, hardly ever missing. Billy was sure there were probably sports that Lenny didn't make look easy, he just couldn't think of any.

Lenny DiNardo made everything he did look easy. Not only that, he made whatever he was doing at a given time look like the most fun thing in the world. It was why Billy had always wanted to be like him, pretty much from the first day they'd met.

"With all the stuff that's been happening lately," Billy said, "I'm pretty sure I'm tough enough, LD."

Lenny gave him one of his no-worries smiles. "I hear you," he said, and then put out his palm so Billy could give him an old-fashioned low five they'd seen in a basketball game on ESPN Classic, one where you just slid your own hand over the other guy's, like you were trying to scoop a dollar bill or something off it.

"If my dad is gonna be like this in the regular season, I don't even want to think about what he's gonna be like in the play-offs."

"We're probably gonna need to wear helmets," Lenny said, "and that's just at practice."

Billy poked Lenny, pointed and said, "Can I put my helmet on now?"

Zeke and the Ratner twins were walking straight at them.

When he was close enough to them, Zeke said, "You guys a little big for swings?"

Neither Billy nor Lenny said anything. Billy had a feeling ignoring Zeke wasn't going to make him go away.

Unfortunately he was right.

"I've been forgetting to ask you something, Raynor," Zeke the Geek said. "You had a chance to work on your tackling lately?"

"Yeah," Bruce Ratner said.

"Yeah," Hank Ratner said.

Billy still didn't say anything. He'd been instructed by Mrs. Marion—*ordered* by her, was really more like it—to stay away from Zeke when they weren't in class.

When she had told Billy that, he had almost said, Yeah, Mrs. Marion, I have to be told to stay out of Zeke the Geek's way.

Only now here Zeke was.

Billy couldn't believe he was looking for more trouble in front of the whole school. But he was Zeke, and trouble was really the only thing he was good at, the way Lenny was good at sports or Ben was good at piano.

Maybe he wasn't scared of Mrs. Marion any more than he was of the other kids in the school.

"Asked you a question, Raynor."

Zeke was standing as close as he could be to the swing Billy was sitting on without actually touching it.

"I've got nothing to say to you, Zeke," Billy said, looking up at him.

What happened next happened fast.

The Ratner twins moved in behind Zeke. Suddenly the rest of the playground couldn't see Billy unless they looked through Bruce and Hank Ratner.

Before Billy could get a better grip on the rope handles attached to his swing, Zeke the Geek leaned down and jerked the seat up so that Billy went flying backward into the dirt.

"Hey," Lenny said, hopping out of his own seat. "That's just plain old wrong, dude."

Zeke turned to him and said, "You want some of this, DiNerdo?"

"Yeah," Lenny said, stepping toward Zeke, "unfortunately, I guess I do."

"Lenny, no!" Billy said, getting to his feet, brushing the dirt off him. "You don't want to get suspended over this loser, too."

"Why not? It'll be fun," Zeke said. "Then we can be losers together."

"Good point, Zeke, no kidding," Billy said. "It's amazing you don't get better grades with a brain like yours."

"You really think I'm gonna let you get away with sucker-punching me?" Zeke said.

"I try not to think of you at all, Zeke."

Billy looked past Zeke. No teachers around, just like the last time.

The only person close to them, he saw, was his brother Ben.

Zeke didn't know he was there yet, because Ben was behind him. There he was, anyway, wanting to see what was going on at the swings.

Billy put his eyes back on Zeke so that Zeke wouldn't wonder what he was looking at behind him.

"Just so's you know," Zeke said. "This still isn't over."

"Boy, there's pretty great news," Lenny said.

"Shut up, DiNerdo."

"Yeah," the Ratner twins said, at the same time.

The twins turned to go. So did Zeke.

Who saw Ben now.

"Hey," Zeke said, "it's little Raynor."

He walked right up to him, put out his hand, the way people did when they wanted you to shake it.

"How you doing, little Raynor?"

Don't do it, Ben.

Don't shake the guy's hand.

Ben put his hand out.

Zeke took it.

Zeke didn't have it long. Billy couldn't hear what he was saying. And knew it didn't matter. However hard he was squeezing Ben's right hand, he didn't let go until Ben yelled, the sound coming out of Billy's brother and somehow just blending in with all the other yells from recess.

Monday night was now the official night of the week when they went out to dinner with their dad.

When their dad had first stopped living with them, their mom had assured them that they would work out some kind of schedule where all the kids would spend regular time with him on weekends. "Quality time," she called it. When Eliza heard that one, she laughed, saying that if she started doing that, it would be the first time she had ever spent quality time with Dad on weekends in her life.

Billy knew something too:

Their dad had never spent much time with Ben on weekends, if you didn't count when the two of them would go to a movie together. Billy had always sort of thought that the movies were their best time together, for both Ben and Dad, because that was a couple of hours when they didn't have to try talking to each other.

Joe Raynor would show up at some of Ben's tennis clinics when Ben was still playing tennis. It was the same with soccer before Ben quit. Sometimes Billy would tag along to Ben's games when his mom was working on a Saturday, just to keep his dad company. So Billy knew better than anybody in the family that Dad had no interest in tennis, even if one of his sons was playing it, and didn't even know the names of the positions in soccer.

Billy had gotten the most of what Eliza called "Dad time."

Lucky me, he thought.

Tonight they were sitting at their favorite table at Bobby Van's, a restaurant all the Raynor kids liked as much for the desserts as for the burgers and chicken fingers, chicken fingers being the only thing

Billy could ever remember his brother Ben ordering when they were out to dinner.

Billy and Ben had gotten into it with Zeke earlier in the day. Afterward, Ben swore that his hand was fine, but Billy wasn't so sure. When they'd gotten home, he'd asked Ben to prove his hand was okay by playing something on the piano in the living room.

Ben said he had studying to do if they were going out with Dad, and to stop bugging him about his stupid hand.

Now they were waiting for their food and their dad was doing the same thing he did at every one of these dinners so far: going around the table and asking each of his children what they'd been doing since he saw them last.

Billy wondered if their dad wrote out what he wanted to do at dinner, the things he wanted to talk about, the way he wrote out what they were going to do at basketball practice.

Eliza went first, mostly because she always did, pretty much giving a play-by-play of her week, both in and out of school. Sometimes when Billy watched his big sister, he pictured her picturing her*self* in one of those real-life MTV shows she was always watching, just without any cameras around.

Billy knew his dad didn't give a rip about what Eliza and her girlfriends had been talking about all week. He still tried to act interested, even throwing in a question once in a while when Eliza would actually stop to take a breath.

After Eliza, it was Ben's turn. Their dad tried to make a joke of it when he explained why they were going out of order, age-wise, saying to Billy, "I know what you've been doing since last week's family dinner—shooting."

"Good one, Dad," Billy said.

His old reliable. Like going to his favorite spot on the floor.

"How's piano?" their dad said to Ben. "Getting ready for the big day?"

"I guess."

Ben seemed more interested in the chicken fingers and fries on his plate, shoveling them in with his head down like the rest of them were timing him.

"C'mon, guy," Joe Raynor said. "You gotta be

more fired up than that. This is what you've been working for."

Still Ben didn't look up. "Whatever," he said.

Their dad, being their dad, wouldn't let it go.

"You should be as fired up about this recital of yours as Billy is about the play-offs."

Ben, like he was talking to his plate, mumbled, "I'm not Billy."

"What did you say?"

Ben looked up, like his eyes were on fire all of a sudden. "I said I'm not Billy. Piano isn't basketball. It's not a team sport. It's just something else I do *alone*."

"But the principles are the same in anything you want to do well," their dad said. "Hard work pays off in the end. You put the work in at practice—"

Ben tossed down his fork, and it hit an open spot on his plate, hard. And loud.

Like Ben's voice now.

Ben said, "This isn't basketball! So why are you pretending you care?"

"If one of my sons is playing the piano, then I care about it," their dad said. "And I know you know that."

But their dad didn't seem so sure about it, at least not to Billy. Maybe this wasn't the way dinner was supposed to go.

It wasn't going like a practice.

"Talk to me, Ben," their dad said.

"I *am* talking," Ben said. "You guys always want me to talk, except when I say something you don't like. Like about you not liking piano."

"Sounds to me as though you're the one who doesn't like piano all of a sudden," Joe Raynor said. "And you want it to be my fault."

This was the stubborn dad really starting to come out now. Billy had seen it enough times himself.

"Why are you acting like this is such a big deal?" Ben said. Even he seemed surprised that he was still yelling this way, in a restaurant, and at his dad. "It's never been a big deal to you, so don't try to make it out like that now. Okay?"

"Don't talk to me in that tone of voice," their dad said, looking around to see if other people were listening. "I was just trying to have a conversation with my son."

"Have it with Billy, then," Ben said.

He pushed back his chair. The chair fell over

behind him, nearly clipping a waiter carrying a full tray of plates. Ben didn't even seem to notice. He just ran for the door.

When nobody else at the table moved, Billy got up and ran after him.

He didn't know he had to be the man of the house even when they went out.

THIRTEEN

The next night Billy's mom came home from work early, gave Peg the night off, made dinner for all three kids herself.

She hardly ever came home early from work and only seemed to be eating dinner with them a couple of nights a week now. Some weeks it was no nights at all. So this was like a special occasion, all the kids even helping to set the table.

Eliza just kept making jokes about their mom preparing the dinner, asking her stuff like, "You can still find the oven and the microwave, right, Mom?"

They had chicken and mashed potatoes and then chocolate ice cream sundaes for dessert. When everybody had helped clear the dishes, Billy announced that he'd worked on his art project in free period and was going into the den to watch a basketball game. Eliza said she was going on her computer until her favorite show came on at nine o'clock.

Ben actually said he was going to practice piano, maybe just as a way of showing Mom he was still into it, even if Billy couldn't tell anymore whether he was or not.

Billy loved his brother, or he wouldn't have stuck up for him the way he did with Zeke the Geek, and he sure wouldn't have covered for him when he skipped piano without telling anybody. And Billy did feel kind of bad that Ben had been in such a grumpy mood lately, about almost everything, even a dinner out with Dad.

But it wasn't his job to take care of Ben. It was his parents' job, even if his parents weren't living in the same house anymore.

He was never going to admit this, especially to his parents, but the only person Billy wanted to worry about right now was himself. He just wanted to play basketball and have everybody else in his family leave him alone.

What he really wanted to do?

Shoot a ball.

His dad was always going to think he shot too much. But as far as Billy was concerned, that was his dad's problem. Billy knew his own game better than anyone. His game was shooting. And if their team was going to win the Rec League championship, he knew he had to *keep* shooting.

It was cold out tonight, but Billy didn't care. He went and put on a sweatshirt and a knit cap and found his ball in the kitchen closet. Then he threw the switch next to the back door that lighted up his own little court at the end of the driveway.

As he was heading out the door, his mom came down the back stairs.

She smiled at Billy then, gave a little pull to his cap and got it away from his eyes. "So how's it going?"

"Fine."

"Things better with your dad?"

The last thing he wanted to do right now was have Mom start one of her big talks with him, about Dad or anything else.

"Fine," he said. "We've just gotta win three

more games and then we'll have what Dad's been talking about all year: one perfect season."

He thought his mom looked almost sad when she said, "It's what we all want, kiddo. I hope you get it."

Not as much as I do, Billy thought.

He went outside to shoot in the night, knowing there was nobody out there to tell him he was shooting too much, nothing else to worry about except putting the ball over the front of the rim just right and through the net.

When you were a shooter, the only person you really had to count on was yourself.

The schedule for the play-offs went like this:

If you won your first game in the quarterfinals, you played the semis the next afternoon. It was the only time you played on Sunday all season.

If you won *that*, the finals were the next Saturday morning. And the finals weren't at the Y. The last game would be in the big gym at the high school.

"I'm in no rush to *get* to high school," Lenny

was saying before their game against the 76ers. "But next Saturday, high school is the only place I want to be."

"One game at a time," Billy said.

"You sound like a certain coach," Lenny said.

Billy grinned at his best bud and said, "That's the meanest thing you've ever said to me."

They were the first ones at the gym. Mr. DiNardo had forgotten it was his day to bring snacks for halftime and for after the game, so he had dropped them at the gym early and then run to the store.

There were no nine o'clock games for the younger kids today, because the younger kids didn't have play-offs. So for a few minutes, Billy and Lenny felt like they had the gym to themselves.

Billy would feed Lenny. Lenny would feed Billy, who couldn't miss. Lenny made jokes. Billy laughed at them, like always, then made another shot, already feeling as if he were on fire.

Mostly he was happy.

He was happy to be here with Lenny DiNardo, happy to have him as a bud, happy that they had a big game coming up at ten o'clock.

Just plain happy for a change.

There was only one problem.

Even if they won their next two games, even if they made it to the finals, their season was over next Saturday.

Then what was going to make Billy feel this happy?

The Magic scored two points in the first quarter.

Two.

Jim Sarni scored a basket the first time they had the ball and then nobody on the team scored another one before the horn sounded ending the quarter.

They missed layups, missed outside shots, missed free throws. They couldn't do anything against the 76ers' zone, couldn't do anything when the 76ers pressed them all over the court. Even Lenny DiNardo seemed to be trying to set a new personal record for turnovers.

Basically, they had forgotten how to play basketball at the worst possible time.

"This is *not* happening," Lenny said when it was 12–2 for the 76ers.

Billy pointed to the boy sitting at the table with the portable electronic scoreboard in front of him.

"Better tell him that," Billy said.

Billy had missed his first couple of shots. He thought he got fouled on the second and said something to the ref. But before the ref could say something back, Billy heard his dad say, "Hey! The ref's not shooting the ball for us, and he's not losing the game."

It was 14–2 at the end of the quarter. Billy thought it should have been worse than that. He stopped shooting after he missed his second shot, just passed the ball and covered his man, promised himself he'd play better the second half. All ten players on the Magic were here today, nobody sick and nobody missing, so that meant he was only playing two quarters.

Meaning this: If he didn't start playing better, if all the guys on the Magic didn't start playing better, Billy had one more quarter left in his season.

When his dad got the whole team around him before the second quarter started, he looked at Billy and Lenny and said, "You guys and the rest of the so-called first unit take a seat. I need to talk to the guys who are going to get us back into the game."

That's just what the second unit did. As badly as Billy's five had just played in falling way behind, the guys off the bench came out smoking, as if the first quarter had never happened.

Jake Lazar was the point guard, Ollie Brown the shooting guard for this unit. They played the way Billy and Lenny usually played together, had expected to play today. They played so well that Billy started to think that they might get to play the fourth quarter today, when the whole season would be on the line.

The score was 20–20 at the half. When they ripped into the orange slices and small Gatorade bottles Mr. DiNardo had brought, Billy noticed his mom taking a seat next to Peg in the stands.

No Ben.

Billy hoped he was at piano for a change but didn't really care, not today. All he cared about was beating the 76ers.

His mom waved at him, held up a hand to show him she had her fingers crossed.

Billy gave her a quick wave back, the kind you gave when you didn't want anybody else to notice.

When they went back on the court to warm up for the second half, for what his dad called "a brand-new ball game," sounding like a TV announcer, Billy still didn't know which five guys were playing the third quarter and which guys were playing the fourth.

But the horn ending halftime sounded and Joe Raynor said, "Same group that ended the first half starts the second."

Lenny made a motion like he was wiping sweat off his forehead. Despite the way they had played, they were still fourth-quarter guys.

Billy and Lenny were sitting next to Billy's dad. Mr. DiNardo had moved down a few seats.

Without looking at them, Billy's dad said, "I hope I'm not making a mistake having these guys on the bench in the fourth."

"You're not," Billy said. "We won't let you down."

"We'll see about that," Joe Raynor said. "Won't we?"

The second team didn't play nearly as well in

this quarter, and the Magic were behind again, by six points, starting the fourth. Billy expected his dad to give him one more big pep talk then, out of what Billy sometimes imagined was like a whole catalogue full of different pep talks for different situations.

But his dad fooled him.

All he said was this: "You guys have worked too hard to lose in the first round of the play-offs. Just go out there and play every single possession on offense and defense as if the whole season is riding on it."

Then he said, "One guy can't win this game. But a *team* can."

It was probably Billy's imagination, he was sure, that his dad was looking right at him when he said the last part.

FOURTEEN

Billy and Lenny brought the Magic back this time.

They brought them back like it was still just the two of them on this court, the way it had been before everybody showed up for the game.

The Y had painted an extra three-point line on their court this year, a much shorter distance than a regular three-point line, but something the coaches thought would be fun for guys their age. When Billy made one from behind that line to finally put the Magic ahead, Lenny did his best imitation of Walt Frazier, the Knicks TV commentator who was always coming up with funny rhymes.

"We are swishin' and *dishin*' now," Lenny said.

The Magic kept the lead into the last minute of the game. But then Zack Fredman, the best player on the 76ers, their center and the tallest kid in their league, amazingly stepped back and made a three-pointer of his own, the first shot that long Billy had ever seen him make, to tie the game.

Forty-five seconds left.

On their way into the huddle for their last time-out, Lenny said to Billy, "You got one more from downtown in you?"

"You know it," Billy said.

Except Billy's dad drew up the last shot for Lenny.

Billy gave a quick look at Lenny, who mouthed the words *Sorry, dude.*

They were supposed to spread the floor, work the clock down the way they usually did in a situation like this. The only thing different this time, as a way of throwing the 76ers off, was that Jim Sarni, the Magic's center, was supposed to do most of the ball-handling out near half-court. The 76ers had gone back to playing man-to-man for most of the second half, and this was the way Billy's dad had come up with to get Zack Fredman away from the basket when Lenny made his move with about ten seconds left on the clock.

On their way back on the court, Lenny whispered to Billy, "Dude, I've got a feeling they're not just gonna let me walk in and get an open look. So if anything happens, be ready to be Last Shot Raynor again."

"Just run the play he wants," Billy said. "*Please*."

The Magic worked the ball the way they were supposed to. Jim Sarni was good with the ball for a big guy, and Zack Fredman didn't guard him that closely, figuring Jim wasn't going to be the one to take the last shot for the Magic, not with both Billy and Lenny still in the game.

With about fifteen seconds left on the clock, Jim threw it over to Lenny on the right wing.

As soon as he did, Zack crossed them up, just dropped back near the basket like he was playing a one-man zone now.

If Lenny drove the way he was supposed to, Zack was going to be waiting for him.

Lenny put his head down and drove, like he was going to make the play work no matter what.

Only he couldn't.

Even when Lenny got a step on the guy guarding him, there was Zack, looking as tall as a tree. It was as if he was daring Lenny to step back and shoot one from the outside, even though outside shooting was the weakest part of Lenny's game.

Jim Sarni was wide open on the left side of the basket, but to get him the ball, Lenny would have had to try to throw it over Zack.

He threw it across the court to Billy instead.

Jim Sarni yelled that he was open. When he did, Billy's guy backed off just enough to give Billy plenty of room to shoot another three-pointer if he wanted to.

Ten seconds left.

Billy had just made this shot, was sure he could make it again. He didn't rush, but didn't hesitate, either, pretending he was out behind the chalk line he'd drawn in his driveway, pretending he was all by himself out there.

The ball felt perfect coming out of his hands.

In his mind, he saw it going through the basket and winning the game.

Almost.

It was just a little long, catching the back part

of the rim instead of the net, bouncing away as the horn sounded.

Overtime.

Billy stood right where he was, still not believing his eyes, like his eyes had played a trick on him, until Lenny grabbed him by the arm and pulled him toward their huddle.

When they got to the huddle, Billy's dad said, "You had the time and the room to get a better shot. It just wouldn't have been a hero shot, I guess."

Billy said, "But, Dad, I had just made the same exact shot a minute ago."

"*We* didn't need a three," his dad said. "But *you* did, apparently."

Because everybody had already played half the game, his dad could play anyone he wanted in the three-minute overtime. He decided to stay with the guys who had just finished the fourth quarter.

Despite missing the last shot, Billy was still in there.

"Play smart," his dad said to them. "And play with heart. You're playing these three minutes for the best reason there is—to keep playing."

The next two and a half minutes were the best

part of the whole game, with no letdown from either team. Lenny scored a basket for the Magic, on a nice bounce pass from Billy. Jeff Wilpon made the first three-pointer of his life. Zack Fredman hit two shots for the 76ers.

Magic by one.

Then Lenny drove to the basket, drew Zack and what looked like the rest of the 76er team to him, fed Jim Sarni for a layup.

Magic by three.

It was the 76ers' ball, thirty-three seconds left, up three points.

Billy's dad called time-out.

"No fouls," he said. "Just play straight-up defense. Then if they miss and we get the rebound, throw it down to our end and run out the clock."

Then he added: "*No* shots. Is that clear? No shots. If they tie us, it'll be because they took the ball away from us."

The 76ers did foul once, but after that they just tore around the court trying to steal a pass or the ball.

With fifteen seconds left, they threw the ball down to Zack. Lenny was guarding him by now.

Zack turned on him and tried a shot he'd been making the whole game, and missed.

As soon as he did, Billy tore down toward their end of the court. Lenny must have been reading his mind, because as soon as he had the rebound, almost without looking, he whipped a long pass that Billy caught up with at the Magic's free throw line.

Clear path to the basket.

Like it was a layup drill.

And a layup would put the Magic ahead by five points.

Billy figured that was just as good as running out the clock.

Took two dribbles, laid the ball up.

And knew the minute he did that he had shot it slightly too hard. You shot the ball enough in your life, even when you were ten, and you knew.

Billy knew.

The ball didn't even touch the rim, just bounced off the backboard to the other side, bounced right into the hands of Zack Fredman, who had appeared out of nowhere to grab the rebound, like he'd broken some kind of speed record to get there.

The 76ers had already called their last time-out. So Zack just wheeled the way Lenny had, almost before his feet touched the ground, and threw a long pass down the court to Eric Dodds, known as Doddsie, the 76ers' best outside shooter.

Doddsie caught the ball, looked down to make sure he was outside the three-point line, let the ball go with one second left.

The whole time it was in the air, Billy had this sick feeling in his stomach, because he was sure it was going in and they were going to a second overtime.

But in rushing to get the shot off in time, Doddsie had flung the ball up there too hard.

It had hit high off the backboard like Billy's layup, no rim at all, and the Magic had won.

Survived was more like it, Billy thought.

He was still staring at the 76ers' basket when he heard his dad behind him.

"Are you finally done taking hero shots now?" his dad said in a loud voice you could suddenly hear all over the gym.

It was just the two of them in this part of the court, and Billy could see everybody else stopping to watch them. Because they sure weren't celebrating with everybody else on the Magic.

"I thought I could just make the layup and put the game out of reach," he said. "I just missed, is all."

"What part of 'no shots' didn't you understand?" his dad said, not lowering his voice, still steamed. "Or are you under the impression that 'no shots' doesn't apply to you?"

And just like that, Billy was sick and tired of his dad taking shots at *him*.

Sick and tired of being picked on, sick and tired of being yelled at because of basketball, sick and tired of his dad talking about this perfect season and then doing everything to ruin it for him.

"Leave me alone!" he shouted back at his dad.

He didn't care who heard. Not the other players, not his mom, not Peg.

Not anybody.

"You ruin everything!" Billy said.

His dad stared at him for what felt like a long time and then said, "Everything except tomorrow's game."

His dad walked away, saying, "Because you're not playing in it."

FIFTEEN

When they got home, his mom said she would talk to his dad about tomorrow's game.

"It won't help," Billy said. "You think he's going to listen to *you* about *his* team?"

"I *am* a pretty good lawyer," his mom said. "Maybe I can change his mind. Let's just give him some time to calm down first."

"How long," Billy asked, "ten years?"

His mom laughed. As she was on her way up the stairs, Billy said, "Mom? Can I ask you something?"

She stopped. "Sure."

"Do you think you and Dad will ever get back together?" he said.

His mom, Billy knew, always thought before she gave him an answer, about anything. She did that now, leaning on the banister with her arms crossed, head tilted to one side.

Her thinking pose.

Finally she said, "I think I have a better chance of changing his mind about tomorrow's game, let's put it that way, kiddo."

"I still don't get it," Billy said, "no matter how many times we talk about how things changed between you guys."

"Sometimes I don't get it, either, kiddo," she said. She smiled one of her smiles that actually made her look sad, then said, "Maybe it's like your team. Maybe we just started having different ideas about how ours should work."

"Dad's way—" Billy said.

His mom finished the sentence for him.

"Or the highway," she said.

Billy went up to his room. He just wanted to be alone. He closed the door and tried to watch *Hoosiers*, his all-time favorite basketball movie, on his computer, but didn't even get close to the part where the shooter in that one, Jimmy, made the shot to win the state championship.

All season long, Billy had dreamed about making that kind of shot, with the clock running down, to win the Rec League championship. And after his dad had walked out, it had seemed more important to him than ever, because basketball seemed like the best thing he had going for him.

Now he couldn't play the game that was supposed to get them to the championship game.

There was a knock on the door.

"Come on in, Mom," he said.

It could only be her. Ben never knocked first, Eliza never did. Not even Peg.

"I talked to your dad," she said. "No go. His mind's made up." She shrugged and managed a small smile. "Again," she said.

Billy Raynor was no crier. But he felt a heat now behind his eyes he wasn't sure he could fight.

"Why is he doing this?" Billy said. "Why is he acting this way toward me?"

"He says he's not the one doing anything. He said the things that have happened lately, you did them to yourself. That you need to understand once and for all that actions—"

This time Billy finished the sentence for her.

"Have consequences," he said.

He took one of his pillows out from behind his head and slammed it on his bed. "I took a couple of dumb shots!" he said. "I'm not in the NBA. I'm ten stinking years old. Everybody in our league takes dumb shots sometimes. It's not a big deal."

"To your father it is," she said. "I'm just telling you what he says. And he says the time to start making you the player he thinks you can become is now."

"You can't get to be a better player if you don't play," Billy said.

His mom leaned against the side of his door. "You want to talk about this a little bit?"

"No."

"You want me to drive you over to Lenny's?"

"No," Billy said, then quickly added, "thank you."

She left and closed the door behind her. Billy lay there on his bed, staring at the ceiling, staring at nothing, but thinking.

Saturday used to be the best day of the whole stupid week.

• • •

It was Lenny who talked him into going to the game against the Pistons on Sunday afternoon.

"I don't care who else wants you there, dude," Lenny said, after showing up at Billy's front door without even calling first. "*I* want you there."

"Not happening," Billy said, shaking his head.

"You're my friend," Lenny said. "And I'm asking you to be there as my friend."

"Do you have any idea how much it will stink, being there and not being able to play?" Billy said. "And having everybody in the whole world knowing why I'm not playing?"

"Dude," Lenny said. "I'm not asking you to do it for *you*. I'm asking you to do it for *me.*"

Billy knew he had lost this debate right there, that there was no way he could refuse when Lenny put it to him like that.

So he didn't.

He went.

He didn't wear his uniform, didn't shoot around with the other guys before the game. Got under the basket and fed them the ball instead. When his dad came over and said, "Good, you showed up," Billy said, "I showed up for the guys." Not even looking at him, just whipping a pass out to Jake Lazar.

"Good," his dad said again, and walked away.

When the game started, he sat as far away from his dad as he could, all the way down in the last folding chair for their team, cheering for his teammates from there.

When he'd see something in the game he thought Lenny had missed, he'd tell him during a time-out. Or motion for him to come over when somebody on the other team was shooting a free throw.

As the Magic began to pull away in the fourth quarter, mostly because Lenny just wouldn't let them cough up their lead, Billy was the loudest guy in the gym and didn't care.

He was cheering as much for himself as the five guys on the court, cheering for one more game, one more chance.

When it was over and the Magic had won, 42–32, Lenny came running over to Billy, smiling, and said, "No worries, right?"

Billy said, "Well maybe I was a *little* worried when you got that incredibly dopey fourth foul."

Then put up his right hand and slapped Lenny the hardest possible five.

"Just trying to keep things interesting, dog," Lenny said.

"Hey," Billy said to him.

"What?"

"Thanks."

"For making things interesting?"

Billy said, "Thanks for everything."

Lenny wagged a finger at him and said, "One more game."

"Oh, *yeah*," Billy said.

Something in his life was going to come out exactly the way it was supposed to.

Nothing was going to get in his way now.

Nothing.

Lenny came over to Billy's after the game, and they played video games until Billy's mom came in and asked if anybody wanted to go into town for ice cream.

Billy and Lenny immediately started chanting *Whoo whoo whoo.*

"I'll take that as a yes," Billy's mom said.

She said she could drop them off at Dreesen's and pick them up in about an hour, she just had a couple of things she needed to do at the office.

Ben asked if he could come along. Billy and Lenny said that was fine with them.

Dreesen's had far and away the best ice cream in town. Everybody in town knew that Gus, the guy who owned the place, came in early every morning, before the sun was up, to make his own ice cream. Billy didn't know how he did it, but he liked Gus's ice cream even better than Ben & Jerry's.

Basically, you never passed up a chance to go to Dreesen's.

They sat in a side booth. Lenny had what he described as a "gigundo" banana split, three different flavors of ice cream. Billy had a root beer float. Ben had a bowl of chocolate with sprinkles. When he chowed through it before Lenny and Billy were close to being finished, he said he was going next door to MacKenzie's to check out the new comic books.

Ben was big-time into comic books, and Mac-Kenzie's was the only place in town that sold them.

Billy told him he and Lenny would meet him over there as soon as they'd finished, but that Ben shouldn't go anywhere else without them.

"I'm basically in charge of not losing you," Billy said to his brother.

"Don't worry," Ben said on his way out the door, "I won't be like your socks. Or your sneakers. Or—"

"Go check out the new *Aquaman* and be quiet," Billy said to him.

While they finished their ice cream, Billy and Lenny talked about every bad thing they were going to do to the Hornets next Saturday. Then they went to find Ben.

Which wasn't hard.

Billy saw him up the sidewalk in front of MacKenzie's, with Zeke Mills.

Saw Zeke laughing as he shoved Ben to the ground.

Billy was already moving toward them when he saw Ben get to his feet and pull back his right hand, like he was actually going to be dumb enough to throw a punch at Zeke the Geek.

Billy ran.

He ran as hard as he could and launched himself the way he had in the playground that day, the first time Ben had tangled with Zeke.

Only this time Billy was launching himself at his own brother.

It was more like a flying bear hug than anything else, but it did the job Billy wanted it to do and put Ben down on the ground before he hit Zeke.

Billy knew that even though Ben was littler and younger, if he had landed that punch, Zeke was going to punch back.

Billy and Ben went rolling on the small patch of lawn in front of MacKenzie's. When Ben twisted around and saw it was his brother who'd brought him down from behind, like a guy catching you from behind in tackle football, Ben yelled, "Get offa me!"

The way he would when they'd be wrestling in the den or the basement over a video controller.

But Billy wouldn't let him up, at least not yet.

He was sitting on Ben now.

"I'm not going anywhere," Billy said. "Not until you wise up."

Zeke Mills waved a hand at them, like he was

bored all of a sudden, and said, "You two whack jobs go ahead and fight each other if you want to. I'm out of here."

Ben, still trying to squirm out from underneath Billy, said, "Are you gonna let him shove me like that and just walk away?"

Zeke had walked up the street by now, on his way to meet up with the Ratner twins.

"What did you think was gonna happen here?" Billy said to his brother. "You were going to be the first kid in the history of the whole town to beat up the Geek?"

"Sometimes you have to hit back," Ben said.

"And maybe hurt your hand doing it? *Real* smart, Ben."

Billy noticed Lenny standing there above them, not saying anything, looking confused, as if this wasn't the fight he expected to have to break up.

"Will you get off me now?" Ben said.

Billy did. They both got up, Ben more covered with grass and dirt than Billy was, having been on the bottom.

"That guy's a jerk," Ben said.

"And everybody knows it," Billy said. "But

you want to know something? You're acting like a bigger one."

He should have been able to catch his breath by now, but he was still steaming mad.

Not at Zeke.

At his own brother.

"You want to take a chance at messing up your hand before your recital, go ahead!" Billy said, yelling at Ben now. "From now on, I'm not stopping you."

Ben said, "I never asked you—"

"Never asked me what? To save you from acting like a little baby? You're right. I did that on my own. I figured it was something I was supposed to do. Sorry, my bad."

He stuck his own hands in his pockets, so he wouldn't be tempted to grab his brother himself and give him a good Zeke-like shake.

"If you don't care what happens to you," Billy said, "well, guess what? Neither do I."

"Fine," Ben said.

"Back at you," Billy said. "You already cost me one game. You're not costing me my championship game, too."

Ben didn't say anything. Suddenly the only sound on Main Street was the sound of the traffic.

"I'm through getting into trouble because of you," Billy said. "You want to screw up your own season, go ahead. But you're not screwing up mine."

SIXTEEN

Billy and Ben barely talked to each other the next few days.

When their mom was home for dinner, she was always trying to get everybody talking to each other at the table. But the only time Billy or Ben would do that now was when one of them was asking the other to pass something.

It was that way until dinner on Thursday night, when Ben announced that his recital had been moved up two hours on Saturday, to eleven in the morning.

The same exact time as the championship game between the Magic and the Hornets at the high school.

"But it's been on the schedule for one o'clock for months," their mom said.

Ben said, "It's because some big pipe burst at East School the other day. The dance kids were supposed to have their show in the gym over there, only now they can't, on account of the pipe bursting and the gym getting flooded. So they have to use the gym at West on Saturday afternoon after we're done, and they need time for their sets or whatever."

It was the most Billy had heard Ben talk—about anything—since his fight with Zeke.

Their mom sighed and said, "So now you and Billy are playing at the same time."

"Sorry," Ben said.

"You didn't do anything, honey. I'm just upset at the situation."

"Well," Eliza said, "it's not *my* situation." She always had to make things about her. "I'm leaving on my class trip tomorrow. At dawn, practically."

Billy ignored his sister, as hard as that was, and said, "So, Mom, what are you going to do?"

Their mom rested her elbows on the table and made her fingers into a church steeple in front of her face, the way she always did when she was concentrating hard on something. "The only sensible plan, since you're going to be at the game with your father, is for me to watch Ben play, and when he's done, for us to get over to the high school as fast as we can. And even if we don't make it, there will be one parent at each venue."

Something made her laugh to herself then.

"What?" Billy said.

"Did I just say venue?" she said. "I make it sound like the Olympics, just for parents with too much going on."

And that would have been a solid enough plan for everybody if she hadn't gotten a phone call early the next morning, right after Eliza left, telling her she had to go up to Boston for the weekend. Some big "development" in the case she'd been working on.

Billy and Ben were eating breakfast when she told them about Boston, with about the saddest face Billy had seen on her since their dad had moved out.

"It can't be helped," she said. "They weren't supposed to need me until Monday at the earliest. But then the judge issued this ruling late last night. . . ." She tried to smile at both of them, then said, "And you guys don't care about any of this, do you? All you know is that now I'm not going to be there for either one of you tomorrow."

Billy tried to help her out. "It's your job, Mom."

Ben didn't say anything, so Billy kept going. "We know how important it is."

"Not as important as you guys," she said. "I *do* love my job, and won't ever apologize for that, not even to—" She held up a finger like she was telling herself to stop right there. "But I love my children more."

She said for them to finish their breakfast, that she needed to call their father and then talk to Peg about tomorrow.

Even after she left the room, Billy and Ben didn't say anything to each other. But Billy knew they had to be thinking the exact same thing: One of them wasn't going to have a parent watching tomorrow.

Billy had an idea which one of them it was going to be.

She was gone a long time. When she came back, she said, "Your father is determined to coach the game." She was looking at Ben. "He says he has a responsibility to all the boys on the team, not just his son. And I have to tell you something, kiddo. I may not be happy with his decision, but I have to respect it."

Billy said, "You're taking *his* side now?"

"I didn't say that. I said I respect his side. And knowing him, I understand it."

"Here's something Dad doesn't understand," Billy said. "We don't need him as much as he thinks we do."

His mom came over and put her hands gently on his shoulder. "You don't mean that."

"Oh, yes I do."

"He's coaching the game, and that's it," his mom said. "Peg will stand in for me at Ben's recital. With our brand-new, handy-dandy digital recorder."

She went over to the table, as if remembering Ben was still in the room, sat down next to him, covered his hand with one of hers. "I am *so* sorry."

"Not a big deal," Ben said.

"But it is a big deal. And if there was some way I could change things. . . ."

She was usually the one with the words, Billy thought.

Just not now.

"Mom," Ben said, staring down at his empty cereal bowl, "it's okay. Really."

They all knew it wasn't.

It was time for the bus by then. Their mom hugged them both a long time, said she'd call as soon as the shuttle landed in Boston. Then she reminded them for about the tenth time that each of them was supposed to call her on her cell tomorrow, Ben after the big recital, Billy after the big game.

Billy was the only one who heard the last part, because Ben was already out the door.

When they got on the bus, Ben went and sat by himself in the last row. He did the same thing on the way home.

When he got inside, he went straight up to his room. It was the first time Billy could ever remember him not stopping in the kitchen first for a snack.

Billy didn't feel like a snack, either.

Instead he went and got his bike out of the garage and, for the first time, rode it the thirteen blocks to his dad's new house.

SEVENTEEN

Somehow the distance between their house and his didn't look so bad when it was just a few inches on a map. It was a lot longer when you actually had to go there, especially when it was this cold out, way too cold to be riding a bike today. The wind was so fierce on Billy's face it was making his eyes water, but that didn't stop him from pedaling as fast as he could. He hadn't called first, knowing his dad would want to know why he was calling.

He knew his dad sometimes took a half day off work on Fridays and hoped this was one of those Fridays.

He came around the corner of Smith Ridge Road and saw his dad's car parked in the driveway.

Billy walked his bike up to the front door and rang the doorbell, thinking for a second how weird that felt, having to ring a doorbell to talk to his own dad.

When Joe Raynor opened the door and saw it was Billy, he said, "Well, this is a surprise."

"I need to talk to you about something," Billy said. "Can I come in?"

"Of course you can," he said.

When they were in the living room, his dad said, "You want something to eat or drink? You must've just come from school, right?"

Billy said, "I need to get home."

It wasn't really true, since Peg didn't even know where he was. But Billy wanted to get this over with, say what he wanted to say and leave.

Mostly because he didn't like it here. He hadn't liked this place the time his dad had brought him to see it, after one of their nights out. He didn't like it now. This wasn't his "other home," as his dad tried to call it, and never would be.

He had all the homes he needed already.

They sat on the couch. On a small desk against one of the walls, Billy saw there were pictures of him and Ben and Eliza.

Another one of them with their dad on the beach.

None of their mom.

"So what's on your mind, bud?" he said, sounding a lot nicer than he had been around the team lately. "Did you come over here to help me draw up some plays for the big game?"

Billy decided to just come right out with it.

"I think you should let Mr. DiNardo coach tomorrow and that you should go to Ben's recital."

It was so quiet in the house Billy could hear the tick of a clock coming from some other room.

His dad said, "Listen, I already talked this out with your mother."

"I know," Billy said. "She told me before she left."

"We decided this was the best way."

"For you, maybe," Billy said.

"It's not your decision to make, son."

Not bud anymore.

Son. Lenny liked to joke about how dads could do that to you sometimes.

Billy had been *son*-ed.

Billy said, "Ben needs you more than the team needs you."

"Is that so?"

"It is," Billy said, "even if you don't want to admit it. We already won once with Mr. DiNardo coaching. We can do it again."

"We're not going to debate this," his dad said. "And I don't want to fight with you. It seems like we've already done enough of that lately as it is."

"I don't want to fight, either, Dad. I just want you to change your mind."

"I made a commitment to your team when I agreed to coach."

In the quiet house Billy said, "What about your commitment to Ben?"

"Ben will be fine."

"No, he won't." Billy got up off the couch, shaking his head, knowing now he had wasted his time coming over here, the way you finally knew you were going to lose a game, no matter how hard you tried.

But he'd had to at least try.

"Ben is Ben," his dad said.

"Actually, he's not," Billy said. "In case you haven't noticed, Dad, Ben hasn't been Ben in a long time."

EIGHTEEN

Their mom called on Saturday morning just as Billy and Ben were finishing Peg's pancakes, Peg having told them that pancakes were the Breakfast of Champions today, not Wheaties.

"Neither one of you needs me around to play your best," Billy's mom said to him after she was done talking to Ben. "Trust your talent. Both of you."

"Mom," Billy said, "stop worrying. We're both gonna do great."

"Is Ben still standing there?"

"No."

"How's he doing?"

Billy took the easy way out. "He's Ben," he said, thinking maybe that's what both his parents wanted to hear, especially when they weren't around.

"Who's taking you to the game?"

"Peg wants to drop me," Billy said, "then take Ben over to West."

His mom wished him luck again, told him she loved him again, told him to give Ben a hug for her, even knowing that was never going to happen, told him to look out for his brother and hung up.

Billy went back upstairs. When he passed Ben's bedroom, the door was open. And Billy could see that even though the recital was still more than two hours away, Ben was already dressed up in his blazer, khaki pants, white shirt, tie.

It was Billy's tie, which made it a little long for him, but Ben had wanted to wear it, anyway. Peg must have just finished tying it for him.

"You ready?" Billy said from the doorway.

They had stopped being mad at each other at dinner last night, just the two of them eating with Peg. Nobody had apologized about what had happened in front of MacKenzie's. Nobody had said anything about not being mad anymore. But Ben had started talking to Peg about what a dork his science teacher was. Mr. Dooley. Billy had said they called him Mr. Drooley when he had him. Ben had actually laughed.

And just like that, things were normal between them again.

"Are *you* ready?" Ben said.

Billy used one of their dad's lines. "I was *born* ready," he said.

He wanted to get a smile out of Ben, wanted to feel better about Ben going off to his recital without their mom. Or maybe what Billy really wanted was to stop worrying about Ben so he could just be excited about being this close to the championship game.

"I'm sorry I lied," Ben said.

"With your piano teacher?" Billy asked. "Forget it. I already did."

"No," Ben said. "About piano. And the recital."

"I don't get it."

"I said I didn't care," Ben said. "But I do."

"I know. We all know. Piano's your thing, just like basketball's mine. You're going to do great today."

They stood there looking at each other then, nobody saying a word, Ben looking more like the little brother than ever in his church clothes, the tie too long for him, his arms too short for his blazer.

Without thinking about it, just doing it, Billy walked over and stuck out his hand to his brother, palm up, looking for a low five.

Ben put his hand on top of Billy's and gave it a regular handshake instead, like you did when you met a grown-up.

"Good luck, dude," Billy said.

"You, too," Ben said.

For a second, it was like neither one of them wanted to let go.

Lenny DiNardo had been inside the high school gym to watch games with his dad plenty of times. But he'd never been on the floor until today.

The place was huge.

Even when he started shooting around with the guys, he kept stopping every minute or so just to take another look around.

Huge.

He finally took a deep breath and reminded himself of something Mr. Raynor had said after practice on Wednesday, their last practice before the championship game:

"The baskets are gonna be the same height as

they are at the Y. The free throw line is the same distance from the baskets. They're still gonna have us playing five-on-five."

Then Mr. Raynor had said, "Basketball is basketball."

It just felt like more today to Lenny DiNardo, maybe because he and Billy had been thinking about this one basketball game the whole season.

Lenny couldn't wait for Billy to get here, so they could both start getting each other fired up the way they always did.

They'd made it.

The championship game wasn't a month away now, or a week away, or three days away, or even tomorrow.

It was starting in twenty minutes.

Mr. Raynor came over to Lenny. "He and Peg must be on their way. I just used your dad's cell to call the house, and there was no answer. I tried Peg's cell, but she must have turned it off already for Ben's recital."

"They'll be here, Mr. R," Lenny said. "I talked to him right after I got up, and he said he wished we could come over to the gym then."

Mr. Raynor said, "If I know Billy, he would have."

Lenny watched him walk back over to the folding chairs the team used as its bench. He watched as his dad handed Mr. Raynor a phone again, saw Mr. Raynor hit the number keys, wait a moment, then shake his head in disgust.

Where were they?

Lenny got into the layup line with the rest of the guys, stopping whenever he got to the end of the shooting line or the rebounding line to give a look at the doors to the gym, then at the big clock at the other end.

Or at Mr. Raynor.

Lenny DiNardo kept doing that until the horn ending warmups sounded, at one minute before eleven o'clock.

Mr. Raynor came walking toward him then. Lenny didn't like the look on his face.

"I just thought to check my messages at home," he said. "There was one from Billy. He's not coming."

NINETEEN

Billy and Peg sat in the fourth row, the last two seats before the middle aisle, where they were sure Ben would be able to see them.

"You called?" Peg said.

"I left a message," Billy said. "He never brings his cell phone to the games."

"You could've gone to the gym and told him."

"I was afraid if I did, he'd change my mind. Dad doesn't change his own mind, but he's *real* good at changing other people's."

"You're sure about this?" Peg said. "Your brother is the fourth one playing. I could still get you over there, get myself back here in time." She patted the recorder in her lap. "And then pray this thing works."

Billy shook his head, staring at the stage. "I'm

staying. I told Ben I was staying. He's not looking out here now and seeing me gone."

"He'd understand if you changed your mind and left," she said.

"I'm his brother, and I'm staying," Billy said.

Peg reached over and gave his hand a squeeze.

Billy looked over at the clock, the same clock he'd look at during practice, wanting it to slow down when they'd be scrimmaging at the end of practice, not wanting the scrimmage to end.

Eleven o'clock, exactly.

There would be other big games, he told himself. He would make sure of that.

The next time he looked up at the clock at 11:02, the gym at West got quiet and the first boy walked up the steps of the stage they'd set up under one of the baskets, sat down, took a deep breath, held his hands above the keys for a second, then started to play.

The next time Billy looked up at the clock, after the third kid—and first girl—had played, it was 11:15.

Billy knew it was all classical music because his mom usually had that kind of music playing in the house when she was there, working or cooking or just reading. He knew, because his mom had told him, that Ben was playing the hardest piece of anybody in the program, something by Mozart.

And other than hearing when somebody would make a mistake, hitting some clunky key and making a clunky sound that was like dragging a fingernail across a blackboard, that was about all Billy knew about the music he was listening to in the gym at West.

But he knew he'd made the right choice.

For his brother.

The audience had finished applauding the girl. It was Ben's turn now. He came walking up the steps, looking straight ahead, his face real serious. He sat down and had to move the bench a little closer to the piano. When he had it adjusted the way he wanted, he turned and looked down to where Billy and Peg were sitting.

Maybe just to make sure.

Billy wasn't sure if you were allowed to do this at a piano recital, but he gave his brother a couple of fist pumps.

Ben smiled.

Billy thought it was for the fist pump and that he would start playing now.

Only he didn't.

He just kept staring out at the audience and smiling, and it was then that Billy heard, "Is this seat taken?"

And looked up and saw his mom.

TWENTY

He and Peg were out the door after the applause for Ben had finally stopped.

Billy didn't know how good the kids coming after Ben on the program were going to be. But from what he'd heard so far, he couldn't believe any of them would come close to his brother, who had blown everybody away.

As Billy had listened, he realized he couldn't tell the difference between his brother's music and what he'd hear on his mom's radio at home.

That's how well Ben had played.

Afterward, Billy applauded harder than anybody, didn't even get embarrassed when he looked around and saw that he was the only one in the gym giving his brother a standing O.

His mom finally touched his arm and said, "Go."

The clock said 11:25.

Halftime.

Maybe.

Before he left, Billy said to his mom, "When did you . . . ? How . . . ?"

She said, "I was on my way to the airport in Boston about ten minutes after I talked to Ben and you. And I will give you all the other details later. But right now you have to go play your game."

Billy changed in the backseat of Peg's car.

Looking in the rearview mirror, she said, "I'm not peeking. But I didn't notice you putting your uniform in the car."

Billy said, "I was wearing it underneath my clothes. Just in case."

Peg said, "Little bit like Superman changing in the phone booth."

Ben was a Superman guy, because of his comic books. Billy had never even watched the cartoon show.

"What?" he said to Peg.

"I'm even older than I think sometimes," Peg said, grinning at him in the rearview mirror. "Now I think I'll just drive."

The clock on her dashboard showed 11:40 when they pulled up in front of the gym, after having stopped at what felt like every single stoplight between West and the high school.

Billy ran up the front steps, through the double doors, past a table in the lobby where some girls he knew from school were selling drinks.

On his way across the lobby, he heard a horn sound.

And hoped it wasn't the horn ending the game, that they hadn't played faster than usual today. Or that they hadn't started earlier than they were supposed to—

No. He was still in time.

They were getting ready to start the fourth quarter.

The scoreboard said the visitors were leading 28–24, but Billy had no way of knowing whether the Magic were the visitors today or not.

The guys were still in the huddle around his dad, who was kneeling.

Billy ran for them like he was going for a loose ball.

"Dad," he said.

The other players turned around and stared. Billy felt like everybody in the gym was staring at him.

Again.

Then Lenny and the guys gave him room.

Joe Raynor, still kneeling, looked up, clipboard in his hand. Billy tried to read his face, not knowing how mad he was.

He sure hoped his dad had checked his messages at home, so at least he'd known why Billy hadn't shown up earlier.

If he hadn't checked his messages at home, maybe he didn't think Billy had even tried to call.

"Dad," Billy said again, but then before he could say anything else, his dad held up his hand.

"Later," he said. "We've got a game to win."

"I know I should have told you myself," Billy said. "But I was afraid you'd be mad."

"I'm not mad," his dad said. And then he did the last thing Billy expected.

He smiled. Then he swallowed hard and said,

"What you did is what I should have done for him. I'm proud of you."

The ref blew his whistle then, came over and said he needed the Magic players back on the court.

"I almost forgot," Billy said. "Are we up four or down four?"

"Down," Lenny said.

Billy's dad was still looking at him.

"You ready?"

Billy grinned. "I was *born* ready," he said.

"Then get in there."

TWENTY-ONE

Billy's dad said one last thing to him as they were breaking the huddle. "Don't be afraid to shoot."

It was Magic ball. Billy could see the Hornets were in a packed-in zone, which is what happened when your team couldn't make anything from outside. They basically dared you to keep shooting from out there.

But on that first possession of the fourth quarter, somebody finally did make an outside shot for the Magic. The first time Billy touched the ball he did exactly what his dad had told him to do: drained one.

Now they were down by two.

At the other end, Lenny snuck in behind Tim Sullivan as he was trying to make a move toward the basket, took the ball away from him, wheeled and started up the court for a two-on-one with Billy.

When the Hornets' guy back on defense cheated over to block Lenny's path to the basket, Lenny passed the ball to Billy, just inside the free throw line. His favorite spot.

He drained another one.

Game tied, just like that.

As he ran back on defense, he saw the double doors to the gym open and his mom and Ben walk through them.

When Ben caught his eye, he gave Billy the same fist pump Billy had given him at West.

Billy, trying to be cool, just nodded.

The Hornets went back to a man-to-man, mostly because of Billy. The two teams traded baskets for a while, Lenny being the first to take advantage of the man-to-man with a layup and a short jump shot. Then with four minutes left, Billy hit his third outside shot of the quarter. The game was tied, 38 all.

Maybe the perfect season was going to end up with a perfect shooting day.

The Hornets—Tim, mostly—hung in there,

though. The Magic pulled ahead by two points with three minutes to go. Then the Hornets got a couple of stops and they were up by two. Billy drained another one. Four-for-four. He was still in the zone, and the game was tied again.

A foul at the other end of the court.

Tim Sullivan made one of two free throws.

Hornets by one.

And then everybody stopped scoring, just like that.

It was as if everybody on the court got nervous all at once. It wasn't any big stuff. Jim Sarni got called for a travel right before he hit a shot that would have put the Magic back ahead. A guy on the Hornets cut the wrong way on Tim and he threw the ball out of bounds. Lenny got fouled, went to the line and missed two free throws.

Then Tim, amazingly, missed two himself.

Magic ball, thirty-two seconds left.

Billy's dad called time-out.

In the huddle, he didn't talk about what was on the line for them. He was all business, saying, "We're gonna hold it for the last shot. Except we're gonna pretend that ten seconds left is the end of the game. That's when we shoot. If we miss, that'll still give us time to foul and send them to the line, where they haven't exactly been stellar lately."

He told them to work it around on the outside while they ran down the clock. When it got under twenty seconds, Lenny was supposed to drive to his left—Lenny was the only kid on the team who could dribble equally well with both hands—and then pass it back to Billy as he came around a double screen from the other side.

All Billy could do was nod.

His dad said, "I'm going with the hot hand. *Yours.*"

In the last game, he was finally Last Shot Raynor.

"Wow," Billy said to Lenny as they walked slowly back on the court, both of them trying to breathe normally.

"The way you always wanted it, dude," Lenny said. "You're gonna be *money.*"

Billy could feel his heart pounding in his chest, the way it did when his dad would get mad and make them run those suicide drills at the end of practice. He couldn't tell whether he was scared or just excited.

Maybe both.

He wished the game were tied, he knew that for sure.

Wished that the worst that could happen if he missed was overtime.

Then he reminded himself that good shooters weren't ever supposed to think about missing.

He wiped the sweat off what was supposed to be that hot hand of his on his jersey.

As they worked the ball around, he touched the ball twice, nearly dropped it right out of bounds the second time.

Twenty seconds left.

At ten seconds, a little later than he was supposed to, Lenny crossed over on Tim and went left.

Billy waited, like his dad had told him to, until Jim set the first screen. Made his move. Jeff picked off the Hornets' guy, who had switched over on Billy.

Billy was wide open.

Money, he thought.

Lenny turned and threw him the ball. Billy took one dribble the way he liked to, looked up, went into his shot, felt his legs and arms coming up together.

Five seconds left.

Everything feeling perfect.

Right up until he passed.

Passed to Lenny DiNardo, who was wide open about three steps from the basket because Tim Sullivan had come running—too late—toward Billy.

Maybe it looked like a shot as Billy let it go. But he was passing all the way, hitting Lenny right in stride, watching from his favorite shooting spot as Lenny released the ball.

Money.

There was no time after the ball went through the basket for Tim to do anything but throw the ball wildly down the court as the horn sounded.

The crazy day got even crazier then, guys running in all directions on the court. Billy felt somebody grab him from behind, thinking it had to be Lenny.

Ben.

Who stepped back now and shot Billy the hardest high five in the history of high fives.

Billy said to his brother, "Hey, watch the hands."

"Yours or mine?" Ben said.

Then Lenny was with them, and he was pounding on Billy, and Billy was pounding on him. Then all the other guys on the Magic piled in, and they were all pounding on each other.

When Billy finally got loose, he turned around and there was his dad.

"That wasn't the play I drew up," he said.

Then he said, "But it sure was a play that great players make."

He smiled at Billy then. A real smile. The biggest Billy could ever remember seeing on him.

"Nice pass," his dad said.

ABOUT THE AUTHOR

Mike Lupica, over the span of his successful career as a sports columnist, has proven that he can write for sports fans of all ages and stripes. Now, as the author of multiple hit novels for young readers, including *Travel Team* and *Heat*, both of which went to #1 on the *New York Times* bestseller list, Mr. Lupica has carved out a niche as the sporting world's finest storyteller. Mr. Lupica's column for New York's *Daily News* is syndicated nationally, and he can be seen weekly on ESPN's *The Sports Reporters*. He lives in Connecticut with his wife and their four children.